DIVER CREED
STATION

Oliver Phipps

Gray Door Ltd.

ISBN 978-1-945530-97-5

CONTENTS

CHAPTER ONE:

SECRETS OF THE PAST

No one could say for certain what had happened. The understanding was that several wars in the late twenty-first century spread rapidly and became a global conflict. Weapons long-stored were brought out towards the end, and the world became ravaged as the conflicts spread out of control.

The catastrophic events of the wars caused millions of deaths and eventually led to the massive and chaotic fall of modern civilization.

The exact reasons for these events mattered little after the collapse.

Those fortunate enough to survive the fall would endure the second round of death due to fallout from weapons used during the wars.

Radiation, along with various types of biological and chemical waste, caused death or sterility. Of those who managed to get through this danger, only a small percentage were able to produce children. Humankind drifted to the very edge of extinction.

For many years, the rudimental struggle of humanity was a basic equation of doing whatever was necessary to live from one day to the next.

With often desperate measures, and after almost a century of questionable survival, humankind slowly began to regain a small but precious hope of future existence. Fertility had slowly returned, and the gradual repopulation of humankind began.

During the third quarter of the twenty-second century, small groups of humanity had emerged in what was once the American Midwest. Of the dominant tribes or groups of this period, three stood out as the most significant.

The worst of the three was the Kaberz. The bond of mutual viciousness connected a variety of blood-thirsty tribes considered Kaberz.

These were the people that cared only about surviving. They would stab anyone in the back if need be. The only thing holding these groups together was the advantage of numbers.

Often, the survival rate inside a group such as this would be almost as bad as being outside a group. Yet, upon gaining status in one of these violent tribes, the survival rate increased. To be a Kaber, one only needed to possess the ability to kill anyone or anything without regard.

Kanzites, on the other hand, were organized and more dominant in numbers than the other groups. They had basic knowledge of old-world technologies, and though the Kanzites were reluctant to become dependent upon the ancient devices, they would use whatever was necessary to survive the hostile world. They were hunters, farmers, and scavengers for the most part. Clannish but still versatile, this group would fight when needed but preferred to avoid conflicts when the opportunity arose.

The smallest but perhaps most respected among the groups were the Neotecz. Within this loose-knit group, many smaller yet still connected tribes existed. These independent clusters often met to trade and communicate discoveries.

Tribes considered to be Neotecz were those that remained completely committed to salvaging and utilizing ancient technologies. Though fewer in numbers, they possessed old-world weapons and tribe-designed weapons capable of extensive damage.

No person joined a Neotecz tribe without a substantial tech offering and the potential to assist the tribe with knowledge of old-world technology. It was the desire of many to be in such a tribe as it meant safety and security. Yet, for many years there was little hope of joining a Neotecz tribe.

In 2195, Redstone, son of Zalto, was exiled to the lower lands. Zalto had lost the highland war and, before his death, sent Redstone out of the highland Kingdom to escape a tribe only described by Redstone as "savages."

Redstone and the remnants of his Neotecz tribe, known as the tribe of "V," moved into the lowlands and united with a Neotecz tribe called the Bronz, which was residing in the remnants of Denver. Together these tribes became known as BVZ United and established dominance over the ruins of Denver.

At the beginning of the twenty-third century, around 2202, rumors began to circulate of a new opportunity offered by the BVZ. Workers of all classes were being recruited.

The rumors also strangely mentioned that no knowledge of ancient technology was required. People were reluctant to believe these rumors as it was well known that Neotecz tribes were miserly in adopting outsiders.

Neotecz had a more militaristic social structure than other tribes and constantly scoured the lands for their coveted old-world weapons or parts of weapons to use for repair. They often had energy sources and methods to repair mobile energy sources such as generators. These items always gave the Neotecz an edge over their smaller numbers and allowed them to be selective in recruitment.

For these reasons, few initially believed the rumors of the BVZ accepting others into their tribe regardless of tech education or knowledge.

Yet, the rumors persisted across the vast lowlands, rumors of a higher living standard, such as running water and heat piped into living quarters.

Then, the recruitment papers began to appear. The list of personnel desired included laborers, security, technical, and almost every respectable line of work imaginable. "Come be a part of the BVZ," the papers stated with a hope that had been unseen for many years.

Slowly at first, people began to move in small groups towards Old Denver. The trip from the lowlands to the high country would be arduous and filled with dangers.

The most significant danger was the Kaberz preying on these groups as they migrated to the BVZ.

A few industrious and brave individuals formed security passages and helped those wishing to make the journey. Migration in this manner became known as traveling the "road of hope." The trip would come at a price, though, and many couldn't afford such protection.

Regardless of the method that one arrived at Old Denver, the sight of BVZ security outposts was joyous to the migrants.

Though a fear of not being accepted by BVZ United persisted for the weary travelers, only those with evidence of Kaber affiliation were turned away from the complex.

Once inside, a series of cleaning, grooming, and medical phases began. The food seemed epicurean for people who had only known basic subsistence. The housing consisted of old-world buildings and rooms that had been repaired as much as possible.

For those with technical skills, the housing would often consist of luxuries such as the rumored running water and piped-in heating.

Altogether, the BVZ complex represented a move forward in a world that hadn't seen this type of progress in almost a century.

The real revelation came after several weeks of orientation and classification for the recruits. Once those accepted into the BVZ had been assigned their jobs, whether in food production or armed security, the secret of the BVZ facility was revealed on a basic level.

The information amounted to this. Redstone and those of the tribe of V that survived the highland war came to Old Denver with various technologies, but more importantly, classified access codes for the old-world government systems.

The Bronz tribe held a fair portion of Old Denver in their possession. One facility they retained and had put a considerable number of resources into holding onto was the Virtua-Gauge facility. This sprawling complex had been carefully sealed up and prepared for storage and nonuse by the old-world government when things began to spiral out of control.

The VG facility had been a tough nut to crack for the Bronz tribe. They had no knowledge of its exact propose but knew for certain it must be a prize to have had so much care put into sealing and securing it.

Almost a century later, thorium-powered, robotic security weapons remained functional and online at the facility's perimeter. A host of carcasses and skeletal remains around the facility reminded all would-be trespassers of the continued danger in trying to enter the secure complex without proper access information.

After retreating from the highlands, Redstone contacted the Bronz officials and began negotiations. Eventually, the tribe of V merged with the Bronz and became the BVZ United tribe.

Now, the gem of the Bronz territories came within reach. With the access codes Redstone brought with him from the highlands, much time and danger were eliminated, and the complex was entered safely.

Thousands of virtual pods were discovered in sealed hibernation states. Most all the equipment was found to be serviceable, with some care and effort. Also, a self-contained power system was found to be repairable and eventually became operational.

As the virtual pods came back online, Redstone moved into a commissioner position over the facility.

The pods offered virtual life experiences in luxurious settings. When a person entered a functional pod, a series of progressive mind-altering steps brought the individual into a receptive position. Then, the person would move into a virtual world and the mind perceived this to be the real world.

Everything looked, felt, and tasted as if the person was there. The consciousness believed, even though the person knew in the back of their mind it was a virtual sequence and their body was in a pod; the reality for the mind was what happened in this virtual sequence.

With this technology, an average person could enter a pod and live a virtual sequence of a twenty-first-century billionaire or many other luxurious sequences that were available.

Commissioner Redstone realized he would need a vast workforce to bring the complex back into its original state of operations. He began putting the word out for all those interested in a new standard of life.

When the people struggling to survive realized this to be a genuine opportunity, they increasingly moved towards Old Denver.

The deal for most common BVZ personnel was seven days of work for seven days of virtual time. The hook was immediate as the new recruits would receive seven days virtual time first.

After a person spent leisure time in a virtual pod, there would be no turning back. They would work hard for seven days to live a life unavailable anywhere else the following seven days.

With this new workforce becoming available, the BVZ quickly began making repairs and establishing a functional social structure.

Areas of Old Denver were reclaimed, and by 2217 the area known as Denver BVZ had become the gem of the western territory.

Rizette Vanson came from a lowlands Kanzite tribe. She traveled to Denver BVZ on the arduous road of hope. Her parents could only afford to send their eldest daughter, Rizette, with her aunt, Leea, who promised to watch over her and assist her in this new opportunity until the rest of the family could travel there.

Though the road of hope had been traversed safely many times previously, Rizette and her aunt would have the unfortunate luck of traveling the rugged old highways during the "Battle of Hope," as it later became known.

Rizette seldom spoke of this harrowing experience afterward, but it made an indelible impression on the girl, who was a teenager at the time.

One thing she would tell from time to time concerned the darkest moments of the battle when no one was sure how it would end. She would relay this story with a few tears when others asked her about the event.

"I lay under equipment, on the ground, watching as the Kaberz attacked again and again. Then, when it seemed the savages would surely break through, I saw a young Neotecz captain draw his sword. He turned and looked back to his men with a face of courage. He yelled out, "For hope!" He then ran out into the mass of Kaber forces. It was the bravest thing I've ever seen. I laid my face into the ground and cried as I've never cried before."

Oray Locke and his family lived close to Old Denver and moved there without much trouble when the BVZ began recruiting personnel.

Though his life was in no sense easy, living near the Bronz tribe meant reasonable security. As the BVZ began to grow and thrive, Oray's family realized this to be a great opportunity and eventually moved into the BVZ when Oray was also a teenager, and around the same time Rizette and her aunt arrived.

Both Rizette and Oray qualified as second-level educated personnel, which placed them in proximity of each other during their later teen years.

The two began dating and were married in 2216. Rizette moved into her position as regulation maintenance officer in early 2217. After a year of actual and virtual training, Oray embarked on his somewhat elite position as a system diver technician later that same year. By 2218, both had settled comfortably into their jobs and marriage.

As an RM officer, Rizette policed the virtual zone. When a regulation was broken or abused, Rizette or another RM officer would respond and initiate the procedures for punishment.

Although punishment for virtual zone infractions was not nearly as severe as one would receive for the same crime in the real world, it did help prevent living personnel who used the virtual zone from getting completely out of hand.

Oray also thrived in his position as a diver technician. Critical repairs could only be made in the virtual zone by living people. This came about as a security measure by the developers. The job had inherent dangers, but Oray spoke little of these to Rizette as he didn't want her to worry.

Having been given better living conditions than the base labor force due to their positions, Oray and Rizette relished their new lives together. Their apartment was of a higher standard than either one remembered growing up as children.

All the workers' living standards were raised in the BVZ zone, and regardless of if you were a second-level technician or basic food preparations personnel, life improved significantly once becoming a part of the BVZ.

But there was something unseen, something that neither Oray nor Rizette had an awareness of.

On a typical day of work, Rizette and her regulation maintenance assistant walked through a virtual light door and into a 1970s Beverly Hills, California virtual sequence.

An unfamiliar sound of rock and roll blared as they spotted a shaggy-looking man standing beside a swimming pool.

The man didn't notice the silent entry of Rizette at first, as he stood gazing at a bikini-clad woman floating face in the pool.

"Serri, Serri, what have you done?" Rizette asked as she walked up to him and gazed down at the woman in the pool.

Serri immediately became startled as he realized he was no longer alone.

"I only hit her once. I swear," he replied nervously, appearing upset but not remorseful.

Rizette pulled a virtual tablet up that hovered in front of her. As she walked around the area, she began entering data into it.

"There's a non-living member of personnel floating face down in your pool, Serri. Once appears to be enough. You know I'm growing a bit weary of seeing your face. What was it last month, you killed another scantily dressed woman with a beverage container?"

Serri began pacing around and seemed nervous.

"Why do you RM officers always call them non-living personnel? Why don't you just call them nonors like everyone else? It's not like they're real."

He paced some more and then continued as Rizette moved around him, busily working.

"And it was a beer bottle," he added as he began following behind her.

She glanced back at him.

"Yeah, that's what it was called, a 'beer' bottle. I hope you've been staying away from the old-world tonics and potions. Like I told you, they were known to have side effects."

"Side effects, what kind of side effects?"

Rizette stopped her data entry and turned to the man with a puzzled expression.

"How about it has the effect of you throwing the bottle and killing a woman?"

"Begging your pardon officer, but both are nonors, you know 'non-living personnel.' They're not alive. They're system-generated people. What's the problem anyway?"

He ran his hands through his shaggy hair and continued pacing around nervously.

"And I didn't mean for that bottle to hit that dancer on the head. Why do they always fall like that? This one just fell into the pool after I hit her. And that dancer, she just fell off the stage. Why do they fall that way?"

Rizette walked around the pool again as she looked over the data. Serri continued following her around as he pleaded his case. She stopped and looked at him again.

"Serri, if you hit a living person out there the way you hit a nonor in here, there's the same chance they will fall and die. You may think this is all controlled by someone at a data entry point somewhere, but it's not; the situations are controlled by calculated odds."

He appeared confused by this statement. Rizette pulled a small pen-like device from her pocket. She pointed the device at the woman floating in the pool and a small light shined on her back. The woman seemed to come back to life. She swam to the edge of the pool and began climbing out.

"Odds, Serri, that's all, calculated odds. Meaning, if you hit a, what did you call her, a 'danzer,' here and she dies from that hit, the same thing could happen in real life."

The man still seemed puzzled.

Rizette began to speak towards her tablet as the woman from the pool picked up a towel and started drying off. She was an attractive blonde woman with large breasts. The bikini barely covered her, and she had a tan indicating she likely wore the bikini more than any other article of clothing.

"Subject, Serri 445. Regulation infraction is violent action against non-living personnel resulting in unintended death. Noted, this is the second violent infraction resulting in an NLP death. Rizette 557 requesting punishment proceedings."

As she said this, Serri stood beside the woman from the pool and appeared to be trying to apologize.

From an unknown location above them, a female voice announced.

"Request from Rizette 557 is accepted. Processing data. Please stand by."

Then, the blonde woman threw the towel on the ground, walked away from Serri, seeming very angry, and spoke as if also talking to the voice.

"NLP 25677 class B companion Cherri Lane requesting transfer."

After she said this, the voice replied quickly.

"State reason for transfer request."

"Violence and abuse," replied the busty blonde.

"Request granted."

With this reply from the voice, the blonde woman seemed to turn into light and immediately disappeared.

"Oh, hey, come on now. Don't... Oh, man!" Serri held his hands up and whined about the disappearance of the blonde.

Another infusion of light brought the presence of a pretty, brunette woman in a small bikini. This woman's breasts were not nearly as large as the blonde woman's. After inspecting the new woman, Serri again began to whine.

"Come on! Are you serious? She doesn't have any boobs." He pointed at the woman's chest in despair.

Rizette glanced over at the brunette but continued her work and made no comment. The brunette stared at Serri with contempt and then quickly replied.

"NLP 27334 class B companion Lesley Rose requesting transfer," and once again, the voice asked.

"State reason for request."

"Verbal abuse," the brunette replied quickly.

"Hey... wait, I was just kidding!" Serri went to the brunette with his arms out in a pleading fashion.

"Request granted."

11

The brunette appeared to become light and disappeared. In her place, a plump woman appeared. She wore a bikini also but was not nearly as pleasing to the eyes in the bikini as the previous two women.

"Oh no... Awww, no...." Serri now held his hands to his head in despair. Rizette laughed a little at this new development.

"You should keep your mouth shut, Serri."

The voice now continued, "Punishment calculations for Serri 445; Six hours jail time; eight hours public service."

Serri appeared to pay little attention to this as he continued to examine the plump new woman with obvious disappointment.

When the voice finished stating Serri's punishment, a bright light appeared, and suddenly a Ford, Model T rolled out from the light and onto the swimming pool. Rather than fall into the water, the antique automobile hovered over the water in midair.

"I cannot believe it." Rizette stared at the old car in frustration.

Noticing the car hovering over his swimming pool, Serri began to whine again.

"What's that? Is that part of my punishment?"

Rizette turned to Serri in disbelief.

"Yeah, Serri. As soon as we get some utensils over here, you're going to have to eat that."

Rizette's assistant laughed about this, but Serri appeared to believe her.

"What? I can't eat that! That's not fair! Look, I just hit her once. You can't make me eat that! I'll report you to Central Control!"

Rizette paid no attention to him. She held her tablet up and spoke again to the unseen voice.

"RM officer Rizette 557 requesting a diver at my location." She paused a second, looking closely at the car hovering over the swimming pool, and then continued.

"You better make it a class A, diver."

A few seconds later, a light door opened, and Oray stepped out.

She looked at him and acted surprised before commenting.

"Well, well, why is it every time I request a class A diver, I get you?"

Oray smiled and walked up close to her.

"Well, I made a deal with the other divers. When a beautiful RM officer needs help, I always get the call."

"Oh yeah, so just how many 'other' beautiful RM officers are you assisting anyway?" She stared at Oray with an exaggerated look of suspicion.

"That's confidential diver information." He gave her a sly look.

"Yeah, well, I'm trying to work here, lover boy."

Oray expressed a somewhat fake expression of shock. "I'm trying to work here too. So, what seems to be the problem?"

Rizette nodded her head at the Model T on the pool. She appeared disappointed in needing to point it out.

"What, that thing? Are you sure that doesn't belong here?" He gazed around at the mansion and obvious opulence.

"Where is here anyway? What is this sequence?"

Rizette glanced at her tablet. "This is, 'late-twentieth-century rock star.'"

"What, rock star? What's that?"

"I'm not eating that! You can't make me!" Serri now injected himself into the conversation.

Rizette gently pushed him back and nodded as if she agreed with him. Oray looked at Serri and held out his hand in a questioning gesture.

As Serri walked away mumbling to himself, Rizette pointed at the Model T.

"Can you please do something about that, so we don't have to make Serri eat it?"

"Well, that might be a decoration or something. I mean…" Oray paused and looked around. "What is that terrible noise? That must be the problem!"

He began walking around as if trying to identify where the rock music was coming from.

"No, I'm fairly certain that noise is supposed to be music. And Serri over there is supposed to be a musician in the musical group that plays that music, which happens to earn them a lot of financial compensation. The problem is that." She again pointed to the old car. As she pointed to it this time, she drew extra attention to the fact the car was hovering over the water.

"Oh, well, it sure looked like some kind of decoration for this…what did you say it was again?"

Rizette glanced at the tablet again. "Late-twentieth-century rock star." She then expressed some annoyance with the situation.

Noticing she'd become tired of playing around, Oray pulled a small pen-like device from a utility belt and, pointing it, shot something that stuck to the old car like bubble gum.

Then, the small blob began to glow on and off with a multicolored radiance.

"Don't worry. We'll have this straightened right out." He then raised his wrist and spoke into a thin band.

"Riley, are you working?"

From the wristband came a reply.

"Yes, sir. I'm working towards you as we speak."

Oray looked at Rizette and smiled coyly. "So, while my assistant makes his way here, how about you and I do some sweet-talking?"

She again gave Oray a look of exasperation.

"Listen, honey, you may have a virtual assistant that you don't need to worry about. But my assistant is a living person, not a nonor. And he's right over there. If I do any sweet-talking with you and he observes it, I'll have a hard time living it down back at headquarters."

Oray gazed over at the man talking with a still obviously disgruntled Serri.

"Yeah, all right, I see your point… Can we at least talk about what we're having for dinner tonight?"

Just as Rizette smiled and was about to comment on this, the door opened on the old car.

"Well, that was certainly a learning experience."

A well-groomed man in plain gray coveralls stepped onto the running board of the Model T. He scanned the area and then jumped the short distance to the side of the pool. Once he stood safely on solid ground, he began brushing small pieces of paper off his shoulders.

"Did you know that in the early twentieth century, people had parades for their heroes? In these parades, the hero or heroes would walk down the streets, or rode, often in an open-top vehicle like this one. Then, the people would throw their garbage out of the windows and on top of their heroes. It really is quite an astonishing event. They called them 'ticker-tape parades.'"

Oray and Rizette stared at Riley in disbelief after he'd said this. Riley returned to brushing the ticker tape off his shoulders.

"So, did you happen to find time to trace the problem at the… 'garbage parade'?" Oray asked a little sarcastically.

"Yes, sir, I did, in fact, trace the problem." Riley then moved with enthusiasm towards the mansion, with Oray following him.

Soon, he stopped beside a bush at the back of the luxurious house.

"Right here, sir." He pointed to the ground.

Oray pointed the small pen-like device downward and again shot a small blob onto the ground. The blob glowed for a few seconds as it relayed Oray's credentials to open an entrance into the main system. Then a light portal appeared, revealing steps going down. Riley stepped down into it, followed by Oray.

After descending a short distance, they stepped onto a running platform around a large cylindrical area. Inside this circular area, glimpses of scenes from the twentieth century could be viewed. For a second or two, the sight of a woman in uniform talking with a man in uniform could be seen. They appeared to be from a war era that Oray knew almost nothing about.

Then, two cars could be seen speeding side by side. A second later, a beautiful blonde woman was smiling with pouty red lips, and photographers were taking pictures. Oray followed him down the various levels, catching glimpses of the scenes from time to time.

Riley stopped in front of a panel and pointed to it. Oray began unlatching the large, slightly glowing box. Riley turned to him.

"So, now that it's safe to talk, sir, have you considered the offer yet?"

Oray glanced at his assistant. He then opened the door on the large box, revealing a massive board with a multitude of small rectangular boxes in rows. As he began to work, Oray replied.

"Well, friend. I've given it some thought. But with no more information than you've given me, it's difficult to decide. Can't you tell me more about it?"

Riley considered his question. "I believe I've told you all I've been advised to tell you at this time, sir."

Oray looked back at Riley with suspicion but continued to work inside the box.

"And you're sure this isn't a glitch?"

"Yes, sir, this isn't a glitch. But as I said, if you reveal anything I've told you topside, the system will present it as a glitch, and you will likely receive a new assistant. Also, you must consider well, sir, because you'll not receive this opportunity again. If you betray the trust and communicate any of this information to anyone outside the protective lower levels, you will never get another offer."

Oray pulled a dark rectangular piece from the panel and examined it. He then glanced at Riley again as if his virtual assistant had a malfunction. As he searched his bag for another part, he began to reply in a humoring tone.

"All right, so basically, since I've become a class A diver, I get this special offer you're speaking of? And the offer is like a group of some sort? But you can't tell me more unless I swear to protect the information involved with this 'tribe' or whatever it is?"

When he finished saying this, he stopped working and stared at Riley expectantly.

"Well, yes, sir, that kind of sums up the situation. I might have used a few alternate descriptions, though, such as 'organization' or 'security policy,' but I suppose, for the most part, you are close."

Oray went back to work and, after a few minutes, closed the door to the panel.

"Riley, I don't want to lose you as an assistant. I like you, and this whole thing is just a bit out of the ordinary."

"I like you too, sir. I realize I'm non-living personnel, but even nonors have basic feeling functions. I'm sorry I can't tell you anything more at this time."

Oray relocked the panel and slowly began to move back towards the upper level.

"I understand why the designers placed all critical repairs into the hands of actual living personnel. I know it was a precautionary measure. I also understand the virtual level is much more extensive than I am aware of. But this... well, it just sounds very strange to me. It doesn't sound like a designer implemented procedure. You say it's not a glitch, so what is it? And why is it so important? You don't want me to decline it, but you can't tell me exactly what it is, other than some type of oath."

As they began to walk back to the higher levels, Riley thought for a few seconds and then replied.

"I, in turn, understand your concern, sir. I would very much like to tell you more, but there's a strict discipline involved here. If you accept the oath, I'm sure you'll eventually find all your answers. You're correct in your assumptions of the virtual level. There are many hazards you've not come close to yet. As a class A diver, you'll be subjected to the massive complexities sooner or later, and I feel this would greatly enhance your abilities to deal with them. Perhaps it may seem odd, considering I'm non-living-personnel. You'll just have to trust me on this."

As they reached the portal stairs and before leaving the security of the lower level, Oray stopped and reconsidered their discussion.

"I'll tell you what, Riley. I'll have some time off after this, and I'll decide during that time. When we come back to work, I'll tell you one way or the other."

This appeared to cause Riley to relax.

"Yes, sir. I'll be looking forward to your decision. And please keep in mind what I told you about my concern for your safety, sir."

"I will, Riley."

They climbed the stairway out of the light portal and arrived back onto the grass behind the mansion. They walked up to Rizette, who stood waiting with the look of losing her patience in the matter.

"So, can I continue with this guy's punishment now?"

From a few steps behind her, Serri began to almost cry and whined in a pathetic tone to her.

"Please don't make me eat that. It's not even possible. Is it?"

"Yeah, it should be ready now. Go ahead and hit it with your initiator."

After he said this, Rizette pulled her small device out and shined the laser-like light onto the old car. A light window opened behind it, and the car rolled back into it, disappearing. In its place, a jail door materialized in the style of the 1970s.

"All right, Serri, it's time to pay your dues." She went to the jail door and opened it. Serri laughed a little as if relieved it wouldn't be necessary for him to eat the old car.

He walked into the jail, and she shut the door behind him.

"You'll leave through the virtual level exit. The door will open when your time is up. You should know the routine by now."

Some remark came from Serri inside the cell, but no one paid much attention to it.

"So, just out of curiosity, Riley, could you explain what could possibly cause a glitch like that?" She stared at Oray's assistant with obvious wonder.

"Yes, well, it's quite interesting actually. You see, the old automobile had a nickname in its day. It was fondly called a 'tin Lizzy' even though it wasn't entirely made of tin."

Riley glanced at Rizette for an instant as if awaiting her response to what he thought was funny. When she continued to stare at him with a blank expression, he went on, seeming a bit embarrassed by the pause.

"Now, the man who just entered the incarceration process for a regulation infraction is living a 'rock star' virtual sequence. Interestingly, the band he is a part of in this sequence has a name very similar to the old automobile's nickname."

With this, Rizette appeared impatient and commented.

"Is this going to take long? I'd like to know the problem, but there seems to be a lot of interconnections."

He expressed some discomfort and, after fidgeting a little, continued.

"No, actually, I'm almost finished. So, as it happens, the band had a popular song with 'jail' in the title. Now, when the man received jail time..."

Riley held his hand out in a manner of waiting for her to make the connections.

"So, the 'thing on the pool' was called a tin Lizzy. The music group Serri is supposed to be a part of had a name very similar. And the group had a popular song with 'jail' in the title."

When she said this, Riley got excited.

"Precisely, and then, you needed to access a late-twentieth-century jail for the man's punishment. This triggered the glitch. The complexities of this virtual level are very extensive. With so many layers of information, these things are bound to happen from time to time."

Rizette smiled a little and quickly aimed her initiator at a marble birdbath about ten feet away. When the light hit it, a virtual door opened as before.

"Well, all I can say is, I'm glad to be in the RM department rather than technical maintenance." She and her assistant then went through the door, and it disappeared behind them.

"Did I not handle that well, sir?" Riley asked.

"Oh, you handled it all right. I think 'glitch facts' just don't excite her as much as she thought they might."

"Yes, I agree. Not everyone has the mind of a diver or his assistant." Riley smiled when he said this. Oray chuckled a little as well, indicating he understood his assistant's intended humor.

Later, Oray and Rizette spoke briefly before going to their exit portals.

"You might want to take it easy on Riley. He's a little sensitive when it comes to interaction with living people, other than me."

She looked at Oray and expressed a bit of surprise.

"I didn't do anything to Riley. Besides that, who's the sensitive one here? Riley is a nonor. Granted, he's a high-level nonor but still a non-living person. You're the living person here, but it sounds to me like you're being a bit sensitive about Riley."

Oray let out a deep breath. "Yeah, maybe I am. I know he's a system-generated person. But as a high-level NLP, he has intricate feelings and can be subject to the same discomfort we feel, at least from what I understand. Plus, he's like a friend to me."

Rizette smiled at him.

"All right, big, baby boy. I'll take it easy on your virtual friend."

He smiled back, and they parted ways into the separate exit portals.

A wisp of mist enveloped them as they seemed to float in midair for several seconds. Though the exit process took around ten minutes, Rizette and Oray, along with all the departing personnel, only sensed a few seconds of time.

Once they regained awareness, a heavy feeling came over them. The pods opened, and now came the slightly painful experience of the outer sense actuators retracting. This blob of sensory enhancing material enveloped the individual after the critical sensory actuators were in place. It accounted for the general senses of the body in the virtual world. When a breeze was felt in the virtual zone or anything pleasant or painful happened to the body in general, this blob provided those feelings.

The real pain came when the critical sensory actuators were disembarked from the body. A skull cap with sensor inducers clasped tightly to the head. To the face, a firmly attached mask was designed for breathing as well as a mouthpiece inserted slightly for feeding and drinking.

An individual entered the pod completely nude for the chest, upper and lower crotch attachments to be snugly affixed to the body. These allowed for sexual sensory enhancements as well as waste disposal. After seven days in the pod, these attachments would come off the body rather painfully.

Various levels of cries rang out throughout the virtual disembarking floor. Rizette had by now reached the point where she didn't cry out as much.

When the attachments pulled from her chest and crotch, she held her cries as much as possible. Still, a sound of discomfort emitted involuntarily from her mouth.

After the removal, she always had to sit for a while to recover from the process.

Once she had regained her composure while sitting in the open pod, she stood up and pulled her robe from a hanger on the wall. Robed, she left the small room, and a cleaning crew came in behind her to begin sanitizing the pod for the embarking personnel.

Rizette met up with Oray, who also wore a robe. They walked along with the other personnel who had recently disembarked the virtual zone. These people all appeared disheartened and sad as they moved towards the BVZ Central zone.

On the other side of the long hallway, the line of people who were about to embark to the virtual level moved past. These people were happy; many smiled as they spoke among themselves. Children laughed and jumped up and down in obvious excitement of going back to the wonderful place for seven days of heaven.

Towards the end of the long hall, they passed workers opening more pods up from their cocoons.

From the thousands of virtual pods at the facility, less than a thousand were being used. Yet as more people arrived at the BVZ zone, more and more pods were opened for use.

Oray watched the workers as he walked past. He briefly wondered about this. The pods and the facility, in general, had been placed in a hibernation state by the people of what was considered the old-world, the world that existed before the collapse and near extinction of humans.

Those people certainly did a great job of preparing it for a secure sleep, as the facility was in good shape altogether after almost a century in storage. He wondered what the people must have thought while putting the facility into the hibernation state. They must have thought they would return. Otherwise, why would they take such a precaution?

At the end of this hall, most of the people separated. Males went through a curtain on the right and females to the left. Once through the curtain, they would remove their robes and place them in a container. Then they would step onto a moving walkway.

As they moved slowly along, a sprinkling of water fell onto them, and they would wash. Oray had once heard from general maintenance personnel that the water would spray down when the facility was new. Now, years later, with clean water somewhat scarce and the facility having been recovered from the storage state, a dribble of water would have to suffice.

Oray and Rizette dressed in locker rooms and moved on to their apartment after completing the disembarkation process.

For advanced tech workers, a higher standard of existence was available. Oray and Rizette had what would be considered luxury accommodations for the time.

Although Oray often found it necessary to plug holes and patch windows in the winter, the heat pumped into the room kept the apartment reasonably warm. They also had running water available. Although it came out in a small stream, the ability to get clean water in one's home was a tremendous advantage for the time.

The day following their regular work schedule, they might walk around the ruins of Old Denver within the secure BVZ zone, being sure not to venture too far as the threat of Kaberz continued to exist.

The two would carefully prod around the ruins to find a nice decoration for their apartment or other small treasure to carry home, as this would always be a thrill for the couple.

As more people entered the BVZ, this became more difficult, and they would need to walk farther to find areas that hadn't been rummaged through already. Nevertheless, life for the two skilled workers represented a quality unheard of anywhere else.

Along with the better living conditions, they would receive additional virtual time. Since much of their time in the virtual zone was spent working rather than leisure, they always received two days of leisure time during the regular seven-day shift. Along with these two days, they were allowed four during their off time.

However, to receive all four days, they would be encouraged to spend some time in the health facility to ensure adequate exercise. Although the virtual pods would stimulate some muscle reaction and minimal body movements, it wasn't considered enough for long-term health needs.

Later, the two were returning from one of their long walks. The ruins of Old Denver loomed all around them, and the sense of being in a massive graveyard always seemed present.

"So, where are we going tomorrow?" Rizette asked.

He examined a small, silver teapot they'd found at an old antique shop the two had discovered and were trying to keep a secret.

They stumbled onto the small shop a month earlier, and it had become their favorite spot. The ancient little store resided quietly between several larger buildings that represented no real value for scavengers. Thus, because of the distance and the location, the two had the little shop to themselves, at least for now.

They would spend hours inside the old shop examining the articles of a time long gone. When they would leave, Oray made efforts to disguise and secure the old store. Rizette would laugh a little as he searched for items to set in front of the door, making it appear insignificant. Yet, she also enjoyed their time there and hoped it would remain their secret if possible.

"Oh, maybe that beach you like so much." Oray finally answered his wife's question after some thought and further examination of their new treasure.

"We should put this in the big room on that little corner table. Don't you think that would be a good spot?"

She examined the tarnished teapot in her husband's hand as their footsteps crunched a mass of long-broken glass from a store window.

"Yeah, that'll be a good spot. I'll try to buff it up some when we get home."

As they made their way through the ancient ruins of Denver, the sun began to set. The weather had become cooler, and Rizette liked the idea of a warm beach for a few days.

That evening, they sat in their bedroom under the small light allowed by the BVZ energy board. Most of the power generated went to the virtual level functions. But due to the success of the virtual pods, more workers came to the BVZ daily. This created more labor to clean and work on parts and various power generation devices. As more power came online, the level of power available for the living quarters increased.

Rizette briefly recalled the tiny light they had when first moving into the apartment. This newer and brighter light enabled her to clean the small silver teapot. As she buffed the tarnished silver, she glanced over at Oray.

He'd become very fond of the old books from the antique shop. Many of these were in the form of sealed containers and were still viewable after removing them from the protective cases. She admired his short brown hair and somewhat "rugged" appearance. Oray was in his mid-twenties. He tried to stay clean-cut, but the lack of decent shaving devices often required him to go unshaven until right before virtual-level entry. Though the pods were designed to slowly remove body hair and other bodily growths at a maintenance level, the more hair on the body, the more painful disembarkation became.

Oray would scan the old books for hours and often showed Rizette an unusual picture. Then, they would try to figure out what the details were. She recalled one occasion when they went over a sportsbook for an entire evening, trying to determine how a game was played. The players wore what appeared to be body armor and played with an odd-looking ball. They read the article and gleaned as much information as possible from the book to understand the game.

She loved this about him, and though they enjoyed the leisure time in the virtual level, she felt he had a zeal for life that many around the

BVZ lacked. Most of the people simply worked and survived for the day they would reenter the virtual pods.

Rizette felt the revival of the virtual pods had been a good thing. But it also meant people were using them as an escape from the real world. This concerned her, and she tried to find as many pleasures as possible in the real world. She didn't want the two of them to become completely detached from the world they must exist in.

The following day, Oray lay on an exotic beach after entering the virtual zone.

"Would you like another drink, sir?" Oray looked up at the waiter holding several colorful drinks on a tray.

"Yeah, let me try one of those. There are no potions in these drinks, right?" He pointed to a tulip-shaped glass with a red frozen mixture and a tiny umbrella hanging from the rim.

"Splendid choice, sir, and potion-free as you requested. I'll only bring virgin drinks to you and the missus." The waiter handed the drink to him and then took his empty glass from the table beside him.

Oray sat up and looked out over the waves splashing on the white sand. Rizette stood in the water almost up to her bottom. She wore a bikini, and Oray admired her beautiful figure. She smiled and waved at him when she realized he watched her. Then, she splashed in the waves some and gazed out over the ocean.

She was a beautiful woman in her early twenties, though not necessarily the type he'd seen in some of the old books. He thought she had more of a practical beauty. She had a nice figure and light brown hair that she wore somewhat short as everyone else did due to the virtual pods. Her face was oval and had a girlish appearance. He liked that about her, though, as it complimented the brilliant mind she had.

Rizette ran back up to the beach and sat in a beach chair beside her husband. She smiled at him and tried to catch her breath as drops of water rolled down her lightly tanned skin.

"This is so beautiful. How could they mess up something like this?"

Oray considered her question. This seemed to be something asked often and by everyone. Usually, this question would come to mind as the remnants of humankind would pass what was left of a beautiful structure, or when they would discover something that must have been very wonderful when it worked.

They would wonder how anyone could ruin such a great life. What caused the wars that eventually led to the diseases and sterility, which almost led to extinction? What could be so bad that the people of the ancient world would allow themselves to destroy this? He didn't know for certain, but he did have an answer that helped him deal with the problem. He finally replied to her.

"I suppose it's a simple thing for us to look at it from this setting and then judge them from a distance. But we really don't know what they were up against. I remember when I was young, we had some chickens that provided eggs for us. Then, one winter, the hens died from the cold and lack of food. We ate them one by one as they died. I'd become very fond of the rooster, but after the hens were gone and we were starving, my father killed the rooster for food. I was mad at him, but I ate just as everyone else did."

He paused briefly as if recalling the bitter memory.

"That was the only year we became that desperate for food. Even though we had times when things were tight, we still came through. I think things can change, and we may not see everything involved with an issue. Just as one year my father had to kill a pet to keep his family alive, and the next year we wouldn't consider such a thing."

Rizette studied him for a few seconds after he said this.

"You've given this more thought than other people, haven't you? Most everyone else just likes to hate the people from the old-world and blame them for everything."

"Yeah, I realize that. I just don't think that's necessarily the best answer; something as complex as a civilization collapse must have many different aspects. And yet, we gaze out over a beautiful virtual ocean and sum it all up to them being fools. Is that really the best response? We blame our ancestors for everything when we only have a fraction of the facts."

Rizette lay down on the beach chair and then replied somewhat casually.

"It seems to work for everyone but you."

Oray laughed a little about this, and then Rizette did as well.

After lying in the sun for a while, Oray said. "I've got to make a decision about Riley before we go back to work."

Rizette turned her head to look at her husband.

"Is he still bringing that up?"

"Yeah, he's still asking me about it. I told him I'd give him an answer when I returned to work."

She turned back towards the sky as if considering the problem.

"He must have a glitch. What else could it be? I mean, why would he keep asking you about it, and why does he only talk about it on the lower levels?"

"He says it's not a glitch. And I'm certain if I present it to Diver Control, I'll lose him as an assistant. He even said if I present it to the Control Department, I'd lose him as an assistant."

Now she sat up. "So, what's the answer? You don't want another assistant, but he keeps asking you about it."

Oray took another drink.

"I think I'm going to go along with it. If it's a glitch, that should bring it out. If not, then I can find out what he keeps trying to say but 'can't' say."

"Ray, if it is a glitch and you do as he wants you to do, there could be some serious consequences. You told me one time there were people in the old world that became lost in the virtual zone. I don't want you to take any chances."

"Yeah, I've considered that possibility. But Riley has been my assistant since I was a trainee. He does good work and has never faltered. The only odd behavior I've ever seen from him is this thing. And he didn't bring it up until I became a class A diver. I know he's only a virtual person, but I've grown to trust him. I don't think he would lead me into any danger."

She laid back down as several nonors in swimming suits strolled by.

Finally, she replied, "I just hope you're right."

They relaxed under the virtual sunset, and Oray slowly drifted off to sleep.

CHAPTER TWO:

THE VAGUE PROMISE

"What did you say this sequence was?" The two walked through a massive mansion. Women with pink and white hair, as well as tiny glowing and flashing outfits, strolled past them laughing among themselves.

Oray watched them with interest as their outfits created quite a visual sight. Their breasts glowed with colors swirling around, and the crotch and butt area of their outfits flashed with various patterns of lights.

"This sequence is, 'early twenty-first-century software tycoon,' sir." Riley also expressed interest in the elaborately dressed women as several more strolled leisurely past.

The two made their way up a grand staircase following the signals from a small handheld device and eventually came to a large room.

In the room were several pool tables and an assortment of video games on large screens along the walls. A huge TV screen was also attached to the wall showing some form of music video.

A man stood in the middle of the room, staring at the floor. He appeared to be about forty years old. He wore wire-frame glasses and an oriental silk robe as well as sandals on his feet.

All around the room were more of the young women in the strange glowing and flashing outfits. A few played games, and others sat on the plush furniture around the room. Two stood by the man and stared at the floor as well.

As Oray and Riley moved closer to the man, they saw a portion of the floor glowing with gradient lines, and every few seconds, the area would flash a bit, and scenes from other times and places could briefly be seen. The area appeared to be around five feet wide, though not by any means symmetrical in shape.

"And there it is!" Oray said, indicating this to be the problem they were searching for. The man turned to Oray and Riley.

"Are you guys here to fix this?"

"Indeed, we are, sir. That is a standard fabric degradation hole. We deal with these things all the time, as well as sequence information glitches, among other things. In fact, the other day, we had a 'major cross sequence straddle glitch.' Very interesting in fact; involved a "garbage parade" if I remember correctly."

Oray glanced over at Riley with a slight smile after saying this and then continued.

"We'll have it sorted out for you as soon as possible."

"Gigi fell in the hole and disappeared. When will I get her back?" The man spoke with apparent despair as he gazed back into the hole.

After giving the man's question some thought, Oray concluded he must be referring to one of the oddly dressed women.

"Well, sir, when a standard-level nonor falls into one of these holes, their characteristic components are generally recycled into new NLPs. From what I have seen here, you have several female companion NLPs, but they all appear to be standard level nonors. Once we have the hole repaired and your sequence comes completely back online, you will receive a replacement NLP. But it won't be the same one you lost."

When Oray said this, the man became quite distraught and on the verge of tears.

31

"You mean, it killed her?"

Now, Oray realized the man was likely nothing similar in real life to the one he portrayed in this virtual sequence. His intelligence level seemed to be quite low, and yet he obviously had a high emotional level in its place. Feeling a bit of compassion for the man, Oray tried to soften his response.

"Well, uhm, she will continue in existence, sir, but in a number of different NLP characters."

This eased the situation some for the man who still stared into the hole as if Gigi might suddenly pop back out, glowing breasts and all.

"She was one of my favorites," the man replied in a very sad tone.

Oray gazed around the room at the many other women, all in a variety of tiny glowing and flashing outfits. He had to turn his back to the man as his face became strained to avoid laughter.

Riley looked at him, and Oray smiled and nodded his head back to the man, now behind him. Riley smiled a little, immediately turned his head down, and put his hand up to his forehead as if scratching it.

"All right, sir, we'll get to work now," Oray continued after regaining his composure.

Riley walked out the door and into the hall with his eyes towards the floor as if searching for something. As he searched the floor, several more of the young women strolled past them. These had bright neon-pink hair, and like the others, their outfits resembled a bikini, but the tops glowed multicolored, and the bottoms presented something of a light show as various random displays flashed.

As Oray watched the two women with interest, Riley found the spot he had been searching for.

"Right here, sir."

He pointed to an insignificant spot beside a large vase. Seeming a bit upset at being distracted from the still visible young women, Oray simply nodded, pulled out his pen device, and shot a small glob onto the floor at that spot.

The glob glowed a few seconds, and then a portal opened, revealing stairs down to the lower level.

Once they were well into the secure lower level, Riley asked Oray with anticipation.

"So, sir, what's your decision?"

Due to the recent exposure to glowing breasts and neon-pink hair, Oray had somewhat forgotten the matter.

"Oh, uhm, well, I've decided to accept your offer, Riley. Even though you can't tell me much about it, I trust you. If you say it's not a glitch and it'll be beneficial for me, I guess I'll have to take your word on the matter."

"That is fantastic, sir. I can't tell you how relieved I am. As time passes, I'm sure you'll become aware that you've made the correct decision."

Riley expressed enthusiasm as he said this.

"All right, I'm sure I will. So, is that it then? Are we all done?"

Riley became very serious. "Oh no, sir. You must take the oath. It's the only way you can have access to the benefits of the creed."

Oray appeared a little perplexed by this, but he'd made his decision on the matter and was determined to see the thing through.

"Well, all right then. You tell me what I need to do. It's not going to hurt, is it?"

Riley chuckled a bit. "No, sir. It'll not be painful. But we do need to locate a C6 junction point."

They walked along and passed several of the C3-6 light-emitting junction points. Oray, now becoming a bit impatient, pointed to the junction points.

"Won't one of these C36's work?"

"No, sir. The C6 junction points have been programmed for the specific interface ability to administer the oath." After passing a few more junction points, Riley found one that he deemed to be the C6 series.

"All right, sir, before taking the oath, I must instruct you on the stipulations and warnings regarding the oath."

He moved directly in front of Oray and took a very serious stance.

"If you betray the creed, you will be immediately disenfranchised from all creed facilities and benefits. All access keys will be eliminated, and every effort will be made to turn your betrayal back onto you as an individual diver. Do not underestimate the potential wrath of the creed or its ability to derail and punish any attempt of malicious exposure. If you understand these stipulations and agree to them, you will be allowed to take the oath. Do you understand and accept the stipulations?"

"Yeah, sure, I agree and understand. Let's go ahead with it."

As Oray said this, he began to second-guess his decision and wondered how long this was going to take.

"Outstanding, sir. Please step into the junction point."

When Riley said this and pointed to the rectangular area with lights streaming up and down, Oray really began to wonder about his decision.

"If I step into the light streams, it'll disrupt the information flow."

"No, sir. As I said, these junction points have been programmed specifically for the oath procedure. The information flow will be moved to other points, and your virtual presence code will be scanned for the creed's records."

Oray hesitated for a few seconds. "Are you sure this is necessary?"

"Sir, this is the highest-level interface for the oath. This method will not only give you access to creed facilities but also a class A creed authorization. Believe me, sir; my efforts are for the sole purpose of providing you with the most benefits available. There may be other methods of taking the oath, but this is designated as the official method."

Realizing this was important to Riley, Oray moved over to the junction point and cautiously stepped into the rectangular area as the lights streamed over and around him. He was apprehensive as he looked up and around with the feeling something might fall on him. Then he turned his attention to Riley.

"All right then, what do I do next?"

"Raise your left hand and place your right hand over your heart."

Oray did as he asked.

"Now, repeat after me... I solemnly swear to protect and defend the creed and all information and facilities designated for creed purposes."

Oray repeated the words but without much enthusiasm.

"I have been instructed on the stipulations involved with the creed, and I understand and accept these as part of my oath to the creed."

He again repeated the words.

"And last of all. I swear to access the creed assets only for creed purposes or when necessary due to diver-related dangers."

Again, Oray repeated the words.

"All right, sir, you're all done with the oath."

Oray stepped out of the junction point and looked himself over to make sure he didn't receive any ill effects from the process.

"Well, I'm glad that's all settled," he said.

"There is one more very important matter, sir. I must give you the access information. You must memorize this information and the procedure necessary for using this information. Are you ready?"

By the time Riley said this, Oray had become quite impatient with the entire matter.

"Yeah, I'm ready. And you did say this was the last thing, right?"

"Yes, sir, this is the last thing. But it is vital that you memorize and protect this information."

"All right, just give it to me."

"Your first keyword is 'Monitor.' You're to use this keyword to access the turnstile as well as other minor interface functions. In the

35

event your virtual code becomes misplaced in the system, simply locate the closest advisor and relay the keyword 'Monitor.' This will allow you to access the turnstile. Once you've done so, you must choose another sequence entry point."

Riley paused now as Oray appeared to be drifting in thought.

"Are you getting this information, sir?"

Oray turned his attention back to Riley.

"Yeah, sure, I'm getting it, Monitor, turnstile, got it."

"Very good, this is vital information." Riley then continued.

"The turnstile is necessary to keep the creed station in an undisclosed and secure position. The turnstile will, however, enable you to access the creed station entry position. When you have entered the second sequence from the turnstile, you must again locate the closest advisor and give them the second keyword, 'Merrimack.' At this point, you will gain access to the creed facilities. Do you have this information memorized and secured, sir?"

"Yeah, yeah, I've got it. So, are we done now?" Oray now began to slowly move in the direction necessary for resolving the fabric degradation problem.

"Yes, sir, we're done. I just want to say I am so glad about this development. I have been very concerned about your well-being, and now I am relieved of that concern."

Riley strolled quickly to catch up to Oray.

"That's great. I'm happy that you're no longer concerned. Now, let's get this problem resolved. We've messed around for too long." Oray found the point of degradation and quickly went to work.

Once Oray took the oath, Riley said nothing more about it. Oray became less concerned about the event, and as the days passed, he thought little about it.

A week later, Oray and Rizette strolled along a trail in the mountains. A stream ran off to their right, and they could see a log cabin farther up the trail. It was another place the two enjoyed during their virtual leisure time.

"So, I've been meaning to ask you about the, you know, the situation with Riley. What ever happened with that?" Rizette tapped a stick on some brush beside the trail as she asked her question. She liked to find a long stick at this location and tap objects as they walked. This somehow made the experience seem even more real.

"Oh, that's all over. I took care of that first thing last week. It's no longer an issue."

Rizette stared at Oray with suspicion.

"Really, so how did you manage to resolve it so effectively?"

"I just did as Riley asked. It was some crazy oath thing that made absolutely no sense whatsoever. It was a glitch. It had to be. I suspect Riley just couldn't identify it. But once I followed through the process, everything went back to normal. He's not said another word about it. I felt pretty sure that was all I needed to do. I'm just glad I didn't bring it up to Diver Control. I really like Riley. It would have been a shame to lose him over such an insignificant little glitch."

Rizette smiled and then let Oray get a little ahead of her. She then tapped him on the behind with her stick.

"Hey, you better watch out!" Oray said as he turned and tried to catch her. She ran around him and, moving quickly, entered the cabin. Once inside, they made love and afterward lay in bed holding each other.

"That seems odd, though," Rizette said. Oray looked down at his wife. Her head lay on his chest.

"What seems odd?"

"The glitch. I mean, why would Riley only show signs of the glitch in the lower levels, where the controllers don't have access?"

He considered this a few seconds.

"I don't know. But the system has some very strange complexities. I think it may have something to do with him being a diver assistant. Who knows? At any rate, the problem appears to be resolved."

She lightly rubbed her husband's chest but didn't reply.

Oray sensed his answer didn't really satisfy her. He brushed her short brown hair with his fingers as he tried to think of a way to put her mind at ease.

"I think what I'll do, though, is when a good opportunity arises next week, I'll bring it up casually to Riley. My guess is the glitch has worked itself out, and he'll have no idea what I'm referring to."

After some additional thought, Rizette finally replied.

"Yeah, I guess so. That might work"

They slowly fell asleep in each other's arms.

As their time off went by, Oray became more confident. The odd procedure endured with Riley was just a glitch. He reassured himself on several occasions that all he needed to do was casually mention the procedure to his virtual assistant. Feeling that the glitch had worked itself out after he followed through with the oath process, Riley would have no knowledge of it any longer.

The following week, Oray found himself in the lower level with Riley and decided the time was right to confirm his suspicions about the glitch. As they stood in front of a control panel, Oray brought the subject up as nonchalantly as possible.

"You know, Riley, I've been thinking about it, and I'm glad I went ahead with that creed thing."

Riley stared at Oray with a puzzled look for a second. Oray now felt his assumption was correct, and Riley had no idea what he spoke about. But then Riley replied.

"You should have no doubt about the decision, sir."

When Riley said this, Oray felt his entire body shudder slightly. What had been a slight smile fell from his face. His heart also seemed to slow in his chest. But the anxiety became increasingly worse as Riley continued.

"In fact, if those other three divers had taken the oath, they might not be drifters as we speak. This is one reason I remained so adamant about you taking the oath, sir. As I said before, I realize I'm not a living person, but as a class B NLP, I have been programmed with a moderate level of synthetic codes for emotion. I felt quite concerned for your safety. With three divers becoming drifters in such a short time, I knew the danger was real."

Oray struggled for something to say. His mind grappled with the new information, and the complete lack of preparation for such an answer became painfully apparent as no response presented itself. After a few seconds, he clumsily moved forward with an awkward response.

"Three other divers, you said three divers have become drifters. Do you mean before the restart? Are you talking about before the long sleep?"

Riley now stared at Oray, seeming even more puzzled than before.

"No, sir. I said they are drifters as we speak. Did you not hear me?"

"Yes, yes, I heard you. I just wanted confirmation." Oray rubbed his head to find another angle. He could see Riley was at a loss to his apparent lack of knowledge on the matter.

"I just want to be sure we're speaking about the same divers. Do you have their names by chance?"

Riley's expression changed now, and he became a little more at ease but continued to express some surprise at Oray's responses.

"No, sir. I'm sure I knew their names before they became drifters. But since they've dropped from the grid, I'm only aware of their absence. I would have thought you knew them, sir, or at least heard about them becoming drifters. Do you not speak of such things with your fellow divers in the real world?"

Oray now realized he needed to find an exit to the conversation before things got any worse.

"Yes, well, there are some things we don't speak much about, Riley."

"I understand, sir. I would normally not say anything about such sad events, but now that you're a member of the creed, there are liberties available to you, as long as you only speak on the lower levels."

"All right, Riley, we'll talk about this later. I believe we should get some work done now."

"Yes, sir."

After disembarking from the virtual zone, Oray moved quickly to find Rizette. When he spotted her, she was rubbing her head, which often occurred and by most people after exiting the pods as the sharp stimulators on the skullcap would cause discomfort after their time in the pods.

"We need to go to our secret place as soon as possible."

She looked at her husband oddly while continuing to rub her head.

"All right, we can go after we get cleaned up. I'll pack a lunch, but why the urgency?" As she said this, they moved past a hologram of Commissioner Redstone. The old holographic equipment caused the image to flicker on and off as he spoke of new power generators coming online and the expansion of territory in Old Denver.

"I'll tell you when we get there."

"Okay, I'll wait until then." She then looked at him again with a puzzled expression as they moved into the separate cleaning stations.

They quickly went to their apartment after getting cleaned up. Rizette packed a lunch, and they put warm clothing on as the weather had become increasingly cooler.

On the way to the old antique shop, they fondly called their secret place, Oray and Rizette passed by a squad of BVZ security forces. Rizette liked seeing these security forces; they made her feel safer.

Oray picked up scraps of wood from inside and around the old buildings as they got closer to the shop.

40

He was very proud of the fact he'd put an antique wood stove from the store back into service. He cleverly ran the stovepipe through the adjoining wall and into a large open area of the building beside the antique shop.

After lighting a small fire and checking for tell-tale smoke signs, he confirmed his hopes that by running the pipe into the old building next to the shop, there was very little evidence of smoke to be seen. In this way, they could have a small fire to warm themselves and not be too concerned about others spotting their special place.

Oray pulled a large piece of debris away from the door, so Rizette could enter. He quickly put the wood he'd gathered inside the door. Then he pulled the debris back up to the door to make the place appear of no worth.

Once inside, he started a small fire, and they settled in for a few hours of quiet time.

Rizette always enjoyed the many small decorative items around the old shop, and Oray would often examine the thousands of old books and magazines that had been sealed for protective purposes. Once he found one that interested him, he would carefully take it from the package and go through it page by page with keen interest. Today, however, their routine would not be the same.

"So, what's all of this about?" She sat down in an old chair that she'd done some work on to make it usable again.

Oray paced about somewhat nervously in front of the woodstove as he considered where to start. He put his hands over it and rubbed them together.

"I spoke with Riley about that oath thing, you know, the thing we thought was a glitch."

When he said this, Rizette immediately took on a serious expression.

"What do you mean, 'the thing we thought was a glitch?' Is that supposed to mean it's not a glitch?"

He didn't look at his wife but instead stared at his hands as he rubbed them over the stove.

"Something is very wrong, Riz. Not only did he remember the oath thing. He also spoke more about it. He indicated there were three divers lost in the system somewhere. He specifically indicated there were three divers who were drifters now."

"What exactly does that mean 'drifters?'"

"It means they've become lost in the virtual fabric and have no exit available to disengage from the system."

"So, what happens to the person in the pod?" She obviously struggled to understand.

"Well, it's not talked about much outside the diver department, but when a diver becomes a drifter, the pod is disconnected from the main virtual deck. Then, it's moved to an isolated area and reconnected. The thought is, no one knows whether the diver is in a good place or bad place, so hopefully, they're drifting in a reasonably comfortable sequence."

Rizette thought of this as the fire crackled in the old stove.

"You never told me that was still a danger. When you mentioned it before, you said it happened in the old world." Rizette sat back in her chair with a concerned expression.

"It's always been a risk of the job. I didn't want to worry you. Until now, I thought the risk was relatively small." He also expressed concern after saying this.

"Maybe that's just part of the glitch. If the glitch is still active, he could be talking gibberish, right?"

Oray paused before answering. He then went to an old chair beside Rizette. He'd previously put some material over the exposed framework to make it usable again. He sat down and stared out into the aged shop. Then he finally replied.

"At first, I thought that might be the case. Maybe it still is. But then I remembered something; when I first came to the diver department, after I'd finished my initial training, I remembered a diver suddenly being gone. I didn't know him very well, but his name was Layton. I didn't think much about it, and the word around the department was that he had transferred.

"Then, about a year ago, a class A diver by the name of Vance seemed to disappear also. I knew Vance a little better, though not well. I asked around, and the other divers said he'd transferred out. No one seemed to know where he transferred to, so one day, I asked a Control officer about him. He checked some records and said it was classified. He then said it wasn't the first time the BVZ council had raided the diver department. He thought Vance was likely involved in some secret BVZ project and living a few doors down from Redstone, or one of the council members."

Rizette studied Oray as he told her this and tried to make sense of the new development. He continued to stare out into the shop at an old-world artifact on the wall.

After a long silence and some thought on the matter, Rizette attempted a comment, if only to ease the tension of a silent room.

"Just because a couple divers transferred out of the department doesn't mean it has anything to do with this thing. Besides, how could anything on the virtual level have that effect on a real person? I mean, the whole reason for the lower level is to protect the real world from the virtual world, right?"

Oray sat silent after his wife asked this. Then he took a deep breath and replied.

"Yes, the old-world designers put the lower level into the system as a barrier. Their concern was mainly the NLPs. All nonors have basic levels of emotion and intelligence. The designers thought this allowed for the possibility of mutiny by the NLPs. So, the solution was to separate the two worlds and not allow the NLPs to make critical repairs necessary in the void of the lower level. This is where the diver came into existence. What really concerns me about this situation is, if NLPs desired to take control of even a segment of their world, the divers would be the bridge needed to do that."

As if a light inside her head went off, Rizette suddenly sat up, indicating she had seen what Oray was getting at. She stared at the floor and thought about her revelation for a few seconds.

"So, what you're saying is..." She paused again as if trying to capture her thoughts and put them into words.

"If NLPs wanted to, for some reason, take over control of the virtual level, or even part of it, they would need to recruit a diver to bridge the gap." She then sat back in her chair, trying to sort out the possibilities of the situation.

Oray rubbed his chin as if also trying to determine where the various pieces of a puzzle went. Finally, Rizette again felt compelled to comment.

"I just can't understand what the purpose would be or how this could be. I mean, I understand the connection, but wouldn't Diver Control be aware of something?"

"I don't have it all figured out either but here is some of what I'm considering right now. Around ninety percent of the virtual personnel have no real awareness of their actual situation. A class C companion NLP can stare at a huge fabric degradation hole and have no idea what it is.

"Yet by necessity, around ten percent do have a higher awareness of what they are and where they are. These are the Control counterparts in the virtual world. Just like Riley is my counterpart, there are various Control counterparts in the system. For example, a class A virtual mayor of a city has a very high awareness of what he is and where he is. He also has high levels of feelings and emotions. He knows he can only exist in the virtual world, and he's programmed to maintain various aspects of the sequence that he is a part of. The reason for this is to help Control identify and deal with a virtual situation when a problem develops. These high-level NLPs are Diver Control's virtual contact elements."

"It's like the two class B companions you told me about in that 'rock star' sequence. You said they requested a transfer, and the system granted one due to abuse by a living person. I believe Riley has the same option if I were to be abusive to him. So, apparently, there are several classes of NLPs that understand pain, abuse, joy, happiness. In fact, Riley stated he was 'concerned' for me."

Oray stood up and went to the stove again. As he rubbed his hands over it, he continued.

"Now, if you were a virtual person with the ability to understand your situation and the situation of the world, you're in, you might think along these lines: 'If I make a deal with a few divers to input the necessary information on the living side of things, we could both have almost unlimited possibilities, because from the lower level almost anything can be done if the right program is downloaded on the Control side of the equation.' So, the higher classes of virtual personnel could create their own worlds in cyberspace, and no one would ever know."

Rizette strained to comprehend this theory.

"Are the virtual personnel even capable of desiring such a thing? I mean, does Riley ever think anything like that?"

He considered Rizette's question before answering. Then, he rubbed his hands over the stove again before replying.

"Theoretically, all virtual personnel with a higher understanding of their situation are designed to be content in their position. Riley never expresses any unhappiness in his position. But he does express the higher levels of emotion and intelligence."

Now, Oray turned to his wife and spoke as if realizing something.

"Just think about this, though, Riz. In the virtual zone, there is almost an infinite space for anything if the information is inserted in the correct manner. The designers were obviously concerned about potential growth occurring without their awareness; otherwise, the lower level wouldn't exist. So, Riley wouldn't need to express anything other than what he is expected to express when he is expected to express it because when he's not being my assistant, he could be the king of some long-forgotten country. He could be doing anything he wants while I'm not around."

She stood up and walked over beside him.

"Are you saying there could be virtual people doing the same thing we're doing, living completely different lives in some corner of the virtual level, completely out of our sight or knowledge?"

He strained at this question.

"I guess that's what I'm saying. I don't know. But I remember Riley saying something about punishment and creed facilities. I didn't pay much attention at the time, but now I'm seeing all sorts of possibilities. He may have been genuinely concerned about my welfare, but the danger may be from some renegade virtual faction that has somehow breached the security blocks. If this is the case, they may either recruit new divers to assist them or cast them out into the virtual wasteland with no hope of returning to the real world. He may have seen my taking the oath as a measure of safety, but now I may be in the middle of a virtual world crime gang. From some of the things Riley said, there seems to be an entire area set aside for this creed, whatever it is."

Oray reached down and put another scrap of wood into the stove. Rizette stood motionless, seeming to be in a mild state of shock. Neither one spoke for a while as both searched for an answer. Then, Rizette said what she often did when trying to solve a problem.

"So, what are our options?"

46

He moved over to a broken-down counter and picked up an oddly shaped antique and began to examine it. Then he replied.

"Right now, there doesn't appear to be many. If I report anything to Control, I may be punished by this 'creed' entity, whatever it is. If I manage to expose it somehow, my code is sure to show up in their database. Or, if by some chance this is just a glitch, we may be worried about nothing."

Rizette replied with concern, "But if it's not a glitch, there could be three divers trapped in cyberspace, with you and me being the only ones that might be able to help them."

When she said this, Oray became obviously distraught and quickly sat the antique back on the old counter.

"Yeah, you're right. That makes this more complicated."

They both walked over to the rough chairs and sat back down. They stared blankly into the small shop as if the ancient artifacts might somehow work their magic again and make them feel better.

After eating some of the lunch and talking it over again, they decided to do some probing to gather more information.

Rizette's aunt was a council member, and though Rizette didn't speak with her very often, she decided to try to visit her. If she could casually ask some questions, perhaps they could get enough information together to make some type of move.

CHAPTER THREE:

A DESPERATE APPROACH

Oray casually stepped up to the large control area and leaned on the counter.

Tal sat behind the monitoring board, moving information items around with the touch of his fingers.

Oray didn't know Tal well, but as the senior controller, he would be the one who may know something in relation to the missing divers.

"Tal, how ya been?"

"Oh, hi Oray. I've been all right. What can I do for you?"

"Well, I've been wondering about something. Do you happen to remember a diver by the name of Vance?"

Oray then gazed over to an old picture on the wall, trying not to appear suspicious to the senior controller. Tal never looked up, though. Instead, he continued to work. As he moved lighted boxes around with his fingers, he replied.

"Sure, I remember Vance. Why?"

"Oh, I just wondered what ever happened to him."

"He transferred out, as I recall. Something of an odd deal; just never showed up one day, and then we got a message from BVZ Central saying he was transferred to another department."

"So, the message from BVZ Central never said what department?"

"No, they just tell you what they want, and I don't ask questions. I don't want to end up in the Health Maintenance Department, shoveling food into an auto dispenser."

Oray chuckled a little when Tal said this.

"Yeah, I understand."

Then he thought he might try for a little more information.

"I would sure like to look Vance up sometime. Is there any way I could find out where he transferred to?"

When he asked this, Tal glanced up at him for a second. He then went back to his work.

"I don't know for certain. You might try the Central Information database. I heard they've got that part of the facility functioning at almost forty percent now."

Oray smiled. "All right, I'll try that. Thanks, Tal."

"Yeah, sure thing. See you."

Sometime later, Oray entered the virtual zone. As he came to the rendezvous point, he felt apprehensive about seeing Riley again.

"Good morning, sir!"

"Good morning." Oray didn't look Riley in the face. Instead, he examined his tool bag. Riley stood by as if waiting for an additional reply. A few seconds later, he attempted to create conversation.

"Was your time off enjoyable, sir?"

"Yeah, it was somewhat enjoyable, and how about you?"

Riley chuckled a little. "Well, I suppose it was enjoyable. But I prefer working with you, sir."

Oray looked at his assistant with suspicion, "Really?"

"Oh, yes, sir. I look forward to our adventures. I quite enjoy the feeling of being productive and solving problems."

Oray finished preparing his tool bag and strapped it on.

"All right, well, let's go solve some problems then."

During the week, Oray responded coolly to Riley. However, he concluded Riley might be able to give him some information that would be considered suspicious outside the virtual zone. He waited for the right opportunity and made his move.

"So, Riley, I've been wondering about something." Oray worked on a panel in the lower level and tried to sound casual.

"Yes, sir, what were you wondering?"

"Well, I think I may know already, but I just wanted to hear your thoughts on the matter. When a diver becomes a drifter, what happens to him or her?"

Riley wasted no time responding in his precise manner.

"Well, if a diver becomes a drifter, the only thing that can be done is for the pod to be isolated yet connected to the umbilical and all life functional systems kept online. Although there are methods of searching for the diver, and in the past, there have been some successful recoveries. However, without an aggressive search from the Control side, this seldom occurs. Unless the diver has assistance from the virtual side of the system, he or she is generally lost in cyberspace for the duration of their life."

When Riley said this, Oray quickly asked.

"By assistance from the virtual side, you mean the creed?"

"Yes, sir. What else would I mean?"

"Oh, nothing. I just wanted to be sure we were on the same page. Go ahead."

"Yes, sir."

"So, if the diver has no help from either the Control or the virtual side, then it is generally thought the diver may be in a comfortable environment or may not be. No one really knows, so to eject him or her from the virtual zone is out of the question. Control can only hope the diver is in a comfortable sequence and that he or she is able to somewhat enjoy the remainder of their life, under such circumstances anyway."

50

Oray thought this might be the answer, but now he was eager to confirm some of the things they only went over briefly in his training.

"And if I'm not mistaken, there's no way known to remove a person from the virtual pods in that situation—I mean, unless an exit is provided for the diver from either the Control side or the virtual side. Without such an exit, you couldn't remove them, and the person would have no hope of surviving."

"Oh, no, sir, you can't just open the pod and remove a person who is in the virtual zone. The entry and exit points are specifically designed to prepare a living person's mind and body for the dramatic change. Although I suspect the entry and exit appear simple to your senses, there is a step-up and step-down process required for the person to survive the entry and exit."

Riley thought for a second.

"Without the proper exit preparations, it would perhaps be as if you suddenly found yourself falling from a thirty-story building. There may be a large safety net at the bottom to break your fall, but your mind and body would instinctively react to the perceived shock of the situation. You would, more than likely, go into cardiac arrest and die before you arrived at the net to realize the situation was not critical. That's why the pods will not open until the person has exited the virtual zone through the proper disembarkation method. No, sir, the only thing that can be done for a drifter in that situation is to isolate the pod and hope the diver is comfortable, wherever they happen to be."

"That's what I thought. But we only went over that possible situation briefly in training. Maybe they didn't want to scare any potential divers away."

Riley chuckled about this, and Oray did as well. He felt sad that he now had suspicions about Riley. He missed their normal working relationship. Riley appeared to sense something but never said anything. Oray was glad when the time came to exit the virtual zone.

The following day, light snow fell as Oray and Rizette casually strolled through the ruins of Old Denver.

"I was able to confirm a few things from Riley."

She turned to him briefly and then turned back to an extremely dirty store window. Ancient clothing hung on morbid remains of mannequins, sagging and falling apart in various places. Rizette examined the remnants closely as if considering the fashion of the ruined women's wear. Without turning from the window, she replied.

"So, what did you find out?"

Oray slowly followed his wife as she peered through the old store windows one by one along the rough remains of a sidewalk.

"A diver could become a drifter in the system without Control ever knowing the exact reason. Once the diver is a drifter, Control generally just isolates the pod and more-or-less forgets about it. Although there have been successful recoveries in the past, Control must exert an extensive search for this to happen.

"Riley seemed to think Control seldom has a desire to do such a search. So, if this was the case and a diver mysteriously disappeared, BVZ Central might simply issue a bogus transfer notice to prevent the other divers from becoming spooked."

Rizette continued to investigate the weathered storefront and long-deteriorated goods while Oray told her this. Then they came under what was left of a protective overhang. An iron bench still appeared solid enough to hold their weight. Oray brushed as much debris off as possible, and they sat down.

The two stared out at the falling snow. Several large deer walked cautiously around a building and down the abandoned street, seemingly not noticing the two. After giving the new information some thought, Rizette finally replied.

"It just seems so hard to believe that some 'virtual, underworld faction' could still be functional after so long."

Oray pulled his hands out of his pockets as she said this. He breathed on them and rubbed them together to warm them. Then, after replacing them in his pockets, he replied.

"I know. But it wouldn't be any different than the rest of the facility. Obviously, the designers felt they would return after a few years. The hibernation state they left the system and facility in appears to have been meant for them to return and resume normal operations after whatever was happening had stopped. But in the virtual zone, no time at all has really passed. A virtual conspiracy between divers and renegade nonors that was in place at the time of the shutdown would just pick up and resume as if no shutdown ever took place."

Rizette considered this briefly.

"I think I'll go talk to Aunt Leea tomorrow. As a BVZ councilwoman, she has access to information that may give us some direction. Maybe I can get some advice without creating suspicion."

He looked at Rizette with a sad expression.

"I'm sorry you're in this with me, Riz. I wish I knew what to do."

She turned to Oray and saw he was very concerned about their situation.

"You did nothing wrong, Ray. If you hadn't taken that oath, you might be lost in cyberspace right now. I don't know what to do either, but I know we can't just leave three people to slowly waste away in virtual pods somewhere. We've got to find out if they're there, and if they are, we've got to try to help them. I'd never be able to sleep if we just left them in there."

Oray smiled a little at his wife's reply. He felt proud that she had such a great understanding of the potential situation.

"Yeah, I wouldn't either. I know if it were me drifting in a virtual sequence somewhere, I would be hoping someone was, at least, trying to get me out."

The following day, Rizette cautiously walked through BVZ Central. The building was slowly being repaired along with the rest of the facility.

As she moved through, she glanced at workers cleaning and repairing old-world desks and equipment. A few technicians hovered around control panels as a test hologram of a beautiful woman flickered. It would appear then disappear due to their efforts with the long-stored equipment.

She walked past the non-functioning elevator and began jogging up the stairs. When she reached the third floor, she passed various reception people and a few workers cleaning the floor. Then, Rizette arrived at her aunt's office and peeked in.

"Rizee, come in. Where have you been?"

She smiled and entered.

She'd not been to visit her aunt for a while, but nothing appeared to have changed: one large window, having been patched up with pieces of other windows, along with faded walls and the ancient picture behind the desk that her aunt said no one could get down.

Compared to many other places, this office was rather nice. The large desk had a marble top and looked to be bombproof. In the portion of the desk where her aunt sat was a touch screen that functioned and gave her access to data retrieval.

Rizette sat down on the backside of the desk, and her aunt pulled a smaller chair up beside her in anticipation of their conversation.

"So, what brings you all the way up here? I'm hoping you've come just to see me!"

Rizette settled into the chair. "I'm sorry I've not come to visit you for a while, Auntie."

"Oh, that's all right, Rizee. I know you and Oray are honeymooning." After saying this, she winked at Rizette.

"Well yeah, I guess so. But we've been married two years already."

"Has it been that long?"

"Yeah, it doesn't seem like it, but it's been that long… But Auntie, I really need to talk to you about something."

Her aunt now became serious. "What is it, dear? Is there something wrong?"

"Well, I'm not sure. It has to do with Oray's job. Something odd happened in the virtual zone."

When she said this, her aunt put a hand up, indicating Rizette should stop talking. She then stood up and walked over to the door. After checking the outside area for anyone close by, she shut the door and locked it. This caused Rizette to feel even more nervous.

Her aunt then went to her desk and sat down behind it. Having a serious expression, she now leaned on her desk in preparation for what Rizette had to say.

"All right dear, go ahead but don't speak very loudly. I just don't want to take any chances."

Rizette glanced back to the door with apprehension before continuing. Then she went on, rubbing her hands together anxiously.

"It may be nothing at all. I don't want to say too much and create a problem if there isn't a problem. But it seems that Oray may have inadvertently stumbled into some old-world corruption inside the virtual zone. He thought his virtual assistant had a glitch when he wanted Oray to go through an odd ritual that seemed to make no sense. But later, his assistant said things that indicated previous divers had become trapped in the virtual zone. Oray recalls two divers who supposedly transferred, and nothing else can be found out about them."

Rizette changed her sitting position as if uneasy about discussing the matter. She glanced at her aunt and then continued.

"We're worried if Oray brings this up to Diver Control and they uncover something, he'll be accused of being a part of it. But there have been things said by his virtual assistant that sound as if he could face harm in the virtual level if he does anything to shine a light on the situation. We just don't know what to do."

Her aunt leaned back in her chair as if in thought. After a few seconds, she leaned onto her desk again and spoke with a hushed voice.

"Rizee, what I tell you now must not be repeated to anyone other than Oray, and he must also understand that it's confidential information."

Rizette nodded and leaned closer to the desk.

"Something is going on in the virtual zone. I don't know if this has anything to do with what Oray is facing, but Councilman Henriys and his entire family disappeared about a month ago. There's been some indication by Commissioner Redstone that he was involved with a virtual zone conspiracy. We think Commissioner Redstone uncovered the plot, and Henriys fled with his family before the commissioner could get a case together."

Rizette sat back now and appeared even more concerned.

"So, this could be larger than something left over from the old world?"

"I'm afraid that's possible. Everyone around here has been worried. We've not been able to say anything to the BVZ public because Commissioner Redstone feels it could create a panic. Commissioner Redstone has also increased his security and requested additional virtual zone authority to locate the source of the problem."

Rizette grimaced at this new information.

"This makes things even more complicated for our situation. If this turns out to be related, it could appear that Oray is a part of it. On the other hand, if Oray brings it up to Diver Control, he could face reprisals from virtual conspirators."

After considering this, Rizette's aunt asked, "But, what sort of reprisals could be taken against Oray?"

"From what he remembers about the discussion, there could be many. The indications seem to be from becoming a drifter in the system to being framed as a conspirator to deflect attention. If this is as it appears and Oray tries to uncover it, the conspirators may fabricate a case indicating him as the sole conspirator."

After hearing this, Rizette's aunt put her hand under her chin. She seemed to be searching for an option. Rizette also sat silently, considering the scope of the problem. Then her aunt replied.

"Let me think this over, Rizee. Give me a day or two. I'll try to find out about the three divers. Come back by my office after a few days, and I'll hopefully have some news for you."

"All right, Auntie, thanks for the help. I just didn't know where else to turn."

"You did the right thing. I'll do what I can for you and Oray."

Rizette smiled and then went over to give her aunt a hug before leaving.

Upon reaching the bottom floor, she noticed the technicians standing back and admiring the now clear hologram of the beautiful woman. She laughed a little as she moved on to the doorway.

As she entered their apartment, Oray stood by a window, working to patch it up better. The apartment held some heat, but years of nonuse had an obvious effect.

The apartments inside the facility had been sealed up tight along with everything else. Compared to other living quarters, Oray and Rizette had it good. After securing a flat board to the part of the window he was attempting to seal up, Oray turned his attention to Rizette.

"Well, what did your aunt say?"

Rizette sat down by one of the vents that expelled a light stream of heat. Placing her hands close to the vent, she rubbed them together.

"She's going to help us. She also told me something that we can't repeat, or she'll be in trouble."

Oray came over and sat down beside her.

"She said Councilman Henriys and his entire family disappeared last month. Commissioner Redstone seems to have some evidence of him being involved in a virtual zone conspiracy. She couldn't say much, but apparently, this creed thing may be larger than we initially thought."

Oray sat silent after she told him this. Then, he leaned forward and rubbed his hands together and close to the vent, also to warm them. After some thought, he replied.

"I'll go to Central Information tomorrow to try to get some information about Vance."

Rizette immediately replied.

"No, don't do that. Aunt Leea is going to try to find out anything else she can. You should be careful right now. We don't know who to trust."

"All right, I'll wait. So, I suppose we could go to the beach while we wait?"

Oray smiled, and Rizette also smiled. Lying on a warm beach sounded much better than waiting in the cold apartment. They went to the virtual pods and, before long, were basking in the warm sun on their favorite tropical beach. For a little while, they could relax and try not to worry.

A few days later, Rizette walked up the stairs to visit her aunt. As she entered the hallway that housed her aunt's office, she noticed several men in security uniforms. The door to her aunt's office stood open, and when she came to it, the men in security uniforms closed in behind her. This forced her to move into the office.

Behind her aunt's desk stood Commissioner Redstone. Several additional security personnel stood on both sides of the commissioner.

"Come in, miss?"

Rizette now felt very nervous when the commissioner asked her name. She gazed around the office, hoping her aunt would appear.

Then, realizing she must answer him, she mumbled, "Rizette, sir."

"Rizette, please come in and have a seat." He pointed to the chair she had sat in a few days earlier. She cautiously sat in the chair.

"Where is Councilwoman Leea?"

Commissioner Redstone sat down behind the desk. He was well dressed and well-groomed, in his forties, or possibly early fifties. He had the appearance of a soldier and of a diplomat. Rizette immediately felt intimidated by his presence.

"I would like to ask you a few questions first, Ms. Rizette. What is your purpose for visiting Councilwoman Leea?"

"She's my aunt," Rizette answered nervously.

"Is that the only reason you've come to see her?"

Now she began rubbing her hands anxiously while struggling to find an answer.

"I uhm, I just wanted to talk with her about something. Do you know where she is now?"

The commissioner eyed Rizette with suspicion. "Ms. Rizette, Councilwoman Leea is missing."

"What? No, I just spoke with her a few days ago. How long has she been missing?"

"She came to my office yesterday. She was asking about some divers that are also suspected to be missing. She had searched the Central Information database and found nothing. She asked me about them. I was unable to help her either.

"Today, she's missing, and no one has located her yet. I sense you know something. You should tell me everything you know so I can get to the bottom of this."

Commissioner Redstone studied her carefully after telling her this.

Rizette felt ill. She wanted to leave but knew she couldn't. She grasped for something to say. She wanted to trust the commissioner but wasn't sure if he could protect her and Oray from the unknown threat.

If the unseen conspirators could get to her aunt, how could he protect her and Oray? Finally, after she felt she must say something, she stumbled forward, trying to say as little as possible.

"Well, uhm, I just wanted her to check on the divers. You see, my husband is a diver."

"Your husband is a diver, and his name is?"

"His name is Oray. He asked about one of the divers, and no one could tell him where he was transferred. So, he checked on the other diver, and it was the same. No one seemed to know anything. I just thought my aunt might be able to find out something."

The commissioner now stared at Rizette as if she were lying to him. When he replied after a long pause, he spoke with a stern voice and continued to stare at Rizette with suspicion.

"Ms. Rizette, 23 years ago, I came down from the high country with access codes given to me by my father. These codes eventually enabled us to revive these facilities and bring prosperity and stability back to the region. But I've been confronted by a faction of people who wish to take that control from my hands. I'll not stand by idle while this faction endeavors to remove what I have worked so hard to build here, do you understand?"

She nodded, indicating she understood.

"I'm going to get to the bottom of this, Ms. Rizette. You should have no doubt of that."

Rizette felt her body trembling and tried to get control. She said the only thing she could think of to deflect his obvious suspicion.

"I hope you can find my aunt soon, commissioner. She's the one that helped me get to the BVZ. The rest of my family is still in the lowlands. She's the only family I have here besides my husband."

Commissioner Redstone continued to stare at her. He appeared to have a strong suspicion that she wasn't telling him everything. Finally, she asked with a weak voice. "May I go now?"

After what felt like a long pause of silence, the commissioner waved in a manner indicating she could go. Rizette got up and tried to walk out the door without expressing her actual fear of the situation.

She held herself together until reaching the apartment, but when she opened the door and saw Oray, she broke down in tears and fell into his arms.

"What's the matter? What's going on?" He moved her to a chair and helped her sit down.

He knelt in front of her and tried to find out what had caused his wife so much despair. She finally calmed down enough to tell him about her aunt and how the situation had taken an almost deadly turn.

"What can we do? The commissioner thinks we're involved somehow. I had to say something. I'm sure he already knows some of the situation, but I don't know how much. If I said too much, he would surely think we're involved. But if I didn't tell him things he may already know, he'll for certain believe we're involved. And my poor auntie, she was trying to help us and now who knows what's happened to her. I'm scared, Oray. I'm getting really scared."

Oray tried to appear confident. He also felt cornered by the recent events, but he didn't want Rizette to know this.

"We just need to remain calm and not do anything out of the ordinary. I suspect the commissioner will be watching us now. If we leave the BVZ, we'll be dead for sure. There's no way we can pay for security anywhere away from here. If we can keep calm, maybe the commissioner will break the case and then see why we couldn't do anything or tell him much."

This plan appeared to calm Rizette somewhat, even though Oray himself felt the odds were now growing against them.

He suggested they go to the antique shop to cheer themselves up. As usual, Oray picked up bits and pieces of wood along the way. The snow was several inches deep, and they moved close to the abandoned buildings to make their walk easier and conceal any tracks to their secret spot.

Once inside, Oray started a fire in the old wood stove. Both tried to do the things they used to do, trying to bring back some feeling of normality. Oray looked through the books, and Rizette searched the shelves for some small items to examine. Soon they both realized it was a useless effort, and both sat by the stove absorbing the meager warmth.

"We have to return to work tomorrow," Rizette said softly as if hoping it would change the fact somehow.

As the fire crackled in the ancient metal box, they sat silently in the shadows of an age long past, wondering how they could endure the time away from each other.

The following day, Oray and Rizette gathered with the other people preparing for virtual embarkation.

These people were cheerful and excited to be headed back to the virtual zone. As they walked towards the pods, Oray clasped Rizette's hand. It was damp and cold from the stress.

Oray tried to think of things he could ask Riley. Maybe he could get some more information that would be helpful. Maybe while they worked in the virtual zone, the commissioner would solve the case, and everything would return to normal.

He reluctantly let go of her hand as she came to her pod. She looked at him with obvious concern. They would likely not see each other for several days.

Then, Oray moved on to his pod. After disrobing, they settled into the reclining seats, and the initial sensor systems closed around them. The pain came but then subsided.

Now the outer sensor system enveloped them like a blob of moist goo. The doors closed, and everything became dark. The flashes of light began that prepared the brain for virtual entry. They faded into the rhythmic trance accompanied by the embarkation of the virtual zone.

CHAPTER FOUR:

BLOOD BRINGS THE DAWN

Rizette woke up in a dark place, all alone. Although she was unaware of it, Oray woke in a similar situation, and a few seconds after, she did. Both found themselves in a large room with only a vague, artificial light, which seemed to have no source of origin.

Oray stood up and looked around and then glanced down at himself. He wore basic overalls like Riley wore. He began walking around and searching for an exit, but there was nothing.

Rizette also found herself in the basic, gray overalls. She moved in one direction and then to another in the dim light but found no way out of the strange, vast room of nothingness.

After a brief search of the area, Oray shouted out. His voice died almost as soon as it left his mouth. Now a fear as they had never known began to take hold of them. Rizette put her hands to her mouth as tears began to roll down her cheeks.

Oray began to breathe heavily as he raced around, searching in vain for anything to help him out.

On the outside, along the virtual pod level, the lights dimmed after the group of people had all entered their pods and were on their way to their individual virtual destinations.

When all became quiet, and no one was left in the area, several men and several security personnel walked quietly down the halls pushing two empty pods in front of them.

First, they entered Rizette's pod chamber. One man turned off the food and liquid valves. He unhooked these lines and then disconnected the pod from the wall. He then plugged the lines and quickly screwed a small device onto the main pod plug. Small lights flashed on the device, indicating it was functioning.

He pushed a lever down with his foot, and the pod lifted off the disposal port and onto rollers built into the underside of the pod. He turned a knob towards the bottom of the pod to close the disposal port and then pushed the pod out the door and into the hall.

One of the empty pods now went into the chamber, and he connected it where Rizette's pod had been.

The same procedure was repeated in Oray's pod chamber. Then, they quietly wheeled away the pods with Rizette and Oray.

Several floors underground and in an isolated area, the men unlocked a door. They rolled Rizette and Oray's pods inside and lined them up beside several other pods along the wall.

They unscrewed the small device on the back of Oray's pod and then connected it to plugs and ports on the wall and in the floor. They hooked the pod up and turned everything back on. Small lights flashed, indicating the pod was functioning normally again.

Then they unscrewed the device on Rizette's pod and plugged it in as they had done Oray's.

They turned the lights out and left the room. The door locked and only the silent darkness and a few tiny lights remained to indicate anything was inside.

Oray saw a light door open. He quickly moved to it in desperation. As soon as he moved through the doorway, he fell several feet and landed in a hole cluttered with debris.

Oray heard gunshots, people yelling, and as he looked around, men and women in uniforms ran past him with small machine pistols in their hands.

He glanced down at himself and realized he wore a military uniform and held what also appeared to be a small rapid-firing weapon. He dropped the weapon and felt his head. He wore some type of helmet.

Chaos reigned not far away and in front of him. His heart began to beat faster as he searched for Rizette.

Meanwhile, a light door opened, and Rizette moved cautiously towards it. Before entering, she inspected it and tried to see into it, even though she knew this wouldn't be possible; she moved closer and then resisted going through the doorway.

Finally, after realizing she had no other options, Rizette moved cautiously through the doorway.

Rizette also fell several feet as soon as she entered the light. She landed almost on top of Oray. When he realized who had landed on him, he shouted for joy and grabbed her in his arms.

She looked much different as she, too, had a uniform and weapon. She glanced around in a daze as she held Oray in an embrace.

"What's going on? Where are we?" she asked with dismay, still holding the small weapon as if she'd not yet realized it was in her hand.

"You two get out of there. Come on before I shoot both of you," a large man in uniform shouted down to them as they both struggled to grasp the situation.

"What's going on, Ray?" Rizette began to tremble as the chaos enveloped her senses.

The man pointed his weapon at them.

"I'm giving you two seconds to get out of there, soldiers."

"Come on, Let's just go, Riz."

He pulled on Rizette to get her on her feet. She stumbled and now seemed to notice the weapon in her hand.

"What's this?" She held the weapon up and looked at it as Oray attempted to help her out of the shallow hole.

"You better get your weapon, soldier. I'm losing my patience with you two wastes of a good uniform." The man appeared to cock his weapon now.

"All right, I got it. It's right here!" Oray picked up the weapon he had dropped and held it up for the man to see.

"If you two don't get a move on, I'll paste you to the ground."

"Come on, Riz. Let's just do as he says." Oray pulled his wife along as she stumbled and struggled in disbelief of her surroundings. This appeared to pacify the large man who Oray thought must be an officer of some sort.

When they climbed out of the shallow hole and began moving forward, Oray noticed the officer moved in a different direction and towards another small group of soldiers.

As Oray helped his shocked wife forward, more soldiers moved past them. They gazed around and saw what appeared to be a war-struck twenty-first-century city. The buildings were damaged by bombs and shellfire. Ahead of them, the sounds of war were very heavy. They could hear gunfire and see laser fire.

They continued to struggle towards the fighting; Oray thought the sequence must be of a mid-twenty-first-century war. The presence of gunfire, as well as laser weapons, indicated this transitional period of weapon technology.

"What's happening, Ray." Rizette began to walk on her own a bit more but still seemed to be in shock.

"I don't know. Something or someone has put us into this... twenty-first-century war sequence. We've got to keep moving, or we may be shot by the soldiers behind us."

They walked ahead for a while. Several armored vehicles sped past them, and more soldiers jogged by. As they slowly came closer to the fighting, both became startled by the ferocity of the battle.

Oray spotted a bombed-out building to their right. He looked around quickly to make sure no officers were in sight.

"Come on." He moved to the building, still holding Rizette, who had not let go of him. The two stepped over debris and cautiously made their way into the abandoned building.

He found a corner where he could spot anyone entering the building but also where they would be less visible.

After helping Rizette sit down, he sat beside her. She moved close to Oray and put her arms around him as a child might do with a parent. He held her and kept his eyes on the bombed-out doorway.

The fighting now sounded very heavy, and he could see the movement of men and equipment outside.

Darkness settled in as the evening turned to night. The flashes and sounds of war accompanied their misery. There seemed to be only one comforting thought. Oray felt glad the weather was warm. He would hate to be in this situation and need to find warmth for him and Rizette.

They said nothing but simply sat for hours in a mild state of shock. He searched in his mind for any possible way out of this place, but there seemed to be no way forthcoming.

Finally, after the battle seemed to settle down some, Rizette said in a quiet voice.

"What are we going to do?"

"I wish I knew," was all Oray could say. They slowly fell asleep in each other's arms.

Oray woke up at dawn. He slid out from under Rizette and leaned her against the wall. Creeping to the door, he scanned the area outside. The sight he beheld was of a war zone and no hospitable place anywhere.

In the direction they had come from, soldiers moved towards him in the distance. In the direction the officer directed them in, he could see and hear fighting several miles away. Overhead, a jet fighter flew by low and towards the battle. He cautiously moved back to Rizette, who had awakened and now sat up watching him.

"It seems we're drifters in a war sequence."

He sat back down beside Rizette.

"What does that mean?" she asked weakly.

"It means our codes are floating in this virtual sequence with no external controls. We're simple mathematical components of this world. If we don't find a way to eat and sleep here, our real bodies won't eat or sleep in the pods.

"Basically, we'll need to find a way to survive here, or our bodies won't survive in the pods."

"But what if we get killed here? Will our bodies die in the pods?" Rizette now sounded even more concerned.

Oray gazed out to the debris-scattered floor as he considered this.

"I'm not sure. We never went over this situation in training. I can only make a guess based on my knowledge of the system."

Oray paused and thought for a few seconds and then went on.

"If we're at a high enough code level in this sequence, then the system should retain our codes for recycling. Some virtual personnel will not be reinstated when they die. Some lower-level virtual personnel simply have their codes scrambled together with other character codes to produce a slightly different character.

"For example, the officer we saw is likely a character that will remain in the sequence. He may get killed in the battle, but the system doesn't register it as an actual death, and he returns to the sequence. Many of the soldiers we are fighting with and against, however, likely have low-level character codes. So, if we shoot one, their codes would be thrown into a soup of other codes, and a replacement would come from that database; but it wouldn't be the same soldier we shot. So, if our codes are mixed into that virtual pot, the system will tell us we're dead, and we'll die in the pods."

Rizette looked at the floor when he said this. She put her arms on her knees and then put her chin on her folded arms. She stared at the floor in apparent thought of the matter.

"So, it seems we must become a part of this sequence to survive. But by being in this sequence, we could still die."

"That's the way I see it."

Oray took a deep breath and continued.

"But whoever put us here may have already determined our fate. Maybe they want us dead, and this is how they plan to do it. Our odds of surviving this sequence for very long seem low. I suppose the best we can hope for now is to have a high enough code level. If we have that, at least we have a chance to stay alive."

"But for how long? How long will our bodies last in the pods even if we find some way to survive here?"

He considered Rizette's question before answering.

"The pods are designed to stimulate muscles on a low level. So, when we move in the virtual zone, our muscles receive low-level stimulation in the pods. The pods also have a hygienic system that works on a basic maintenance level. This and other maintenance aspects of the pods will slow the degradation of our physical bodies.

"But the real question is how much it will slow the process down. Eventually, our bodies wouldn't be able to survive the debarkation process. At that point, we could live a while longer in the virtual zone, but no matter what, we won't last as long in the virtual zone as we would normally. My guess would be several years before we would be unable to leave the virtual zone. After that, we may survive two to three years longer before our bodies would die."

They thought about this a while but soon realized they must eat. Both were hungry. Oray suggested they try to blend in and maybe find a field kitchen.

"Don't forget your weapon. You may need it, and besides that, the officer seemed to be very upset last night when I almost forgot mine."

Rizette turned around and picked up the small automatic weapon. It felt strange in her hands. She hoped she would never have to use it. Even killing virtual people seemed frightening.

Realizing they both had holsters on their hip, the two put their weapons in them and left the bombed-out building.

A small group of soldiers and a few tanks rolled by as Oray and Rizette got onto the road, moving in the direction of the battle. As they got closer to the place where most of the fighting from the previous day took place, they saw mangled bodies and wrecked implements of war all around.

Rizette cringed and pulled Oray close as the sites were almost too much for her. Again, jets flew over them, low and loud.

"We sure gave 'em hell last night!"

A soldier moved up beside the two. His uniform was weathered, and he had a rough appearance.

"Yeah, we sure did." Oray attempted to sound tough. Rizette let go of him and tried to look unaffected by the carnage all around her.

"Do you happen to know where we can get something to eat? We didn't get a chance to eat last night, uhm, due to killing so many of the enemy."

The rough soldier peered at them with interest for a few seconds. Then he seemed to accept what Oray said.

"Sure, I saw the mobile ration dispenser go by a few minutes ago. I'm looking for it myself. It should be up here somewhere."

The three walked about a half-mile past more bombed-out buildings, dead soldiers of their own, as well as the odd, black-uniformed bodies of their apparent enemies.

The morning sun slowly brought light but remained behind a mass of clouds.

Finally, they came up to a vehicle sitting on the side of the road. More soldiers were gathered around it. The dingy gray color of the vehicle matched the soldiers' uniforms. A black star with lines radiating from four points was painted on the side, and Oray thought this must represent the organization or country they were fighting for.

He and Rizette stood behind the others as they pulled a small round object hanging from the front of their uniform up to a round device on the side of the vehicle. When they did this, the round device on the vehicle recognized the round item attached to the soldier's uniform.

Oray glanced down to his uniform and then Rizette's. They both had the small round button-like objects attached to their uniforms. Once the soldiers did this, a small screen lit up, and they would touch an item on the screen. Then a slot would open, and the rations they chose would be delivered to them.

After observing for a few minutes, Oray decided they would try it. The process proved simple, and soon, he and Rizette were sitting on the remains of a burned-out transport vehicle eating the rations. Oray watched Rizette with a heavy heart as she slowly picked the food from the package with a disposable utensil. She finished the small portion of food and then looked up at Oray. He tried to smile, and just as she was about to smile, someone yelled something.

An explosion erupted close by. Oray caught a glimpse of a black jet zooming overhead, and another explosion rocked them. He grabbed Rizette's arm and pulled her towards the side of the road, where he spotted a low drainage ditch.

Again, a black plane flew over, and more explosions came immediately after. They both fell and then rolled into the ditch. Another black jet flew by low and fired some type of rapid-firing gun that decimated the ration vehicle as it attempted to drive away.

Oray held his body over Rizette as another plane flew over, and more explosions went off close by. He then caught a glimpse of two gray jets flying over. They seemed to be in pursuit of the black ones. A few seconds later, another gray plane zoomed overhead in the direction of the others. Then nothing except the fires and wounded could be heard.

As Oray moved from the top of Rizette, he could hear her crying. He began to break down himself, and several tears dropped onto the back of her uniform. He struggled to restrain the emotional crash going on inside him. He didn't want Rizette to see him like this. He held her as if trying to support her, but he also feared she would turn and see his weakness. He laid his face on her back and fought the fear and anguish inside, then squeezed her tightly. They lay in the ditch for thirty minutes or more.

During this time in the ditch, Oray began to falter inside. He wanted to be strong for Rizette, but inside he felt hopeless.

They both resisted moving due to exhaustion and despair. Troops, tanks, and armored vehicles moved by, and the battle in the distance became fiercer as they lay in the dirt.

A medic stopped to assist them. Oray nodded to tell him they were just resting. Slowly the movement of war slowed, and the battle sounds faded farther and farther away. They still didn't want to leave the makeshift foxhole.

"Get up, you pukes. You're too far behind. Get on up to the front!" a loud and commanding voice rang out over the two. Looking up, they saw another officer who appeared different than the previous officer but similar in demeanor.

"Come on, let's go." Oray helped her up, and they trotted towards the sounds of battle.

As they moved closer to the battle, Rizette sensed a pattern. Eventually, they found a place to stay for the night, and she considered the day's events. Oray slumped beside her, and both finally slept, though lightly.

The next day, she focused on her theory. She watched closely as they moved and stopped. She then began to move and stop to see if her assumption was right. She noticed that they could get close to the battle, and there would be few officers. The fighting appeared to be undertaken by common, lower-ranking soldiers.

Then, she had Oray wait with her by the road for a while. As she watched the activity, Rizette realized there was always a mass movement of soldiers when attacks came close to the front. After this, there would always be a space where only a few soldiers and occasional vehicles moved towards the battle. Then, after around forty-five minutes of this slower activity, the officers would show up. They would shout and threaten to shoot the soldiers lingering around to get everything moving again.

She became a little excited by this discovery but didn't say anything to Oray just yet. As they found a building to sleep in that evening, she considered the situation and felt more hopeful. She wanted to be sure about it first, though. She didn't want to get Oray hopeful as well and then find out she was wrong.

Their bed for the night would be on a hard floor, among dirt and debris—an old curtain to cover them and some wadded plastic sheeting for their pillow.

Rizette watched outside the building and realized as darkness settled in, the battle around them subsided slightly.

The next day, Rizette moved the two along with the battle. To eat, she noticed they needed to get closer to the actual fighting. But she also noticed if they would locate the ration vehicle, get their rations and then move away from the vehicle, they could stay out of the attacks that often came. Over the next several days, she became very focused on this process and didn't notice Oray had become more and more despondent.

She began to tell him about the process, and he would nod and follow along when she said they should move. When she said they should stop, he would do so.

After about a week of this, she concluded there was indeed a "safe zone" around the battle, which they could survive in. If they followed the flow of the battle in this area during the day, they could stay out of the direct fighting but still not face the wrath of the officers. When she told Oray this, she became more enthusiastic about their chances of survival. As they prepared for the night, she tried to explain the plan to him.

"So, we just need to move every day with the army. We can stay in the safe area behind the battle but in front of the officers. We'll need to get closer to the fighting to eat, but then we can hang back to stay out of any possible attacks."

Oray nodded and continued to stare at the floor of the bombed-out store they had chosen to sleep in. She studied him for a few moments. He'd become very discouraged.

She felt good that they now had a chance to survive from day to day. Oray, however, appeared defeated and hopeless. Rizette realized she needed to find some way to encourage him. She just didn't know how or what could do that. No one could blame him for feeling down in this place. But she needed his help if there was any way out of this. They would need his skills as a diver in the virtual zone. She lay down and decided to try to encourage Oray every chance she could.

The next day, Rizette began showing Oray in detail the process of moving within the safe zone. She knew the routine well as this is what they had been doing for some time now. She wanted Oray to see the details of the plan, so he could move naturally rather than her telling him every time they needed to move or stop.

"All right, let's go." Rizette had to more-or-less pull Oray along as if he were a child. They went up to the mobile ration dispenser. She now had a definite pattern of where the food would be distributed every day.

She wasn't certain yet, but there seemed to be a random pattern to the attacks on the dispenser. Often, they would get their food and hurry away from the dispenser. Then nothing would happen.

At first, she thought the pattern was every other day. Then, for three days in a row, the ration dispenser got attacked at some level by various methods. Planes, tanks, and a heliocraft all attacked the dispenser during those three days, not long after they moved away from it.

Rizette tried to get Oray enthused about the small discoveries. But as weeks in this sequence turned into a month, with little progress other than survival, his attitude grew darker and darker.

"Come on, Ray. I need your help here. What should we do now? We have the survival part covered. There must be something else we can do to try to get out of here."

He picked at a small package of food as Rizette said this.

"There's nothing we can do, Riz. We're stuck here." His voice contained defeat and despair.

"Don't say that!" Rizette stood up and paced angrily back and forth in front of him. "I'm tired of you acting this way. I need your help. You act as if there's no hope, but as long as we're alive, there's hope." She stopped and looked down at him. He continued to pick at the food inside the small container.

She walked over to the corner of the building where they had set up their sleeping spot and then sat down and watched Oray. The flashes and sounds of the battle in the distance seemed to frame her husband with dire foreboding. She studied him for a while as his face would light up from the distant explosions. She almost wanted to give up too. But now, she realized that if they both gave up, there would be no hope at all. She lay down and went to sleep with the constant sounds of battle as her comforter.

Several days later, they received their evening rations from the dispenser. They walked a short distance from the dispenser, and Oray sat down on a piece of debris to eat. Rizette scanned the area nervously.

"I think we should get a little farther away," she said.

Oray looked around. "This is far enough. We'll see the attack if it comes and have time to get away." After saying this, Oray immediately went back to eating. Rizette continued to scan the area with apprehension.

"I told you, the attacks on the dispenser are set in a random mode. I don't think we've seen all the different types of attacks yet. If it's one we know about, then we're far enough, but the attacks may come in ways we're not familiar with yet."

He said nothing but continued to eat. Then he finally replied.

"We've been here a month now, Riz. I think we've seen all the different types of attacks."

He no sooner got these words from his mouth when something began hitting all around them.

At first, they didn't know what it was. Then, as Rizette and Oray looked towards the dispenser, soldiers in black uniforms ran into the area, attacking the gray soldiers with weapons firing.

Oray barely turned to his wife in time to see several bullets violently slam into her chest and obviously penetrate the body armor she wore.

In his mind, everything started moving in slow motion. He struggled to comprehend the sight of his beloved Rizette stepping back and falling from the impact of the shots.

A primordial shout of rage erupted from his mouth as the food instantly dropped from his hands. He jumped up to catch her as she fell backward. At this angle, he couldn't remain on his feet as he caught her. They fell together, with her landing on top of him. He slid her over and saw her dead eyes staring into the sky.

Rage erupted inside him instantly as another scream escaped his mouth. He looked up at the soldiers in black moving his way, and a hate as no other brought his blood to a hot boil. Anger as he'd never felt before flowed through his veins as he held his lifeless wife.

He reached over and pulled his weapon from the holster and fired at the soldiers. They began to fall as he aimed and shot them one at a time. Their bullets riddled all around him, but he didn't care if he died or not. Only killing as many of them as possible seemed to soothe his anger.

After fifteen or so fell, a clicking sound came from the weapon. Now, a few more of the soldiers came running from the positions they'd taken cover in. He tossed his weapon aside and, reaching over, pulled Rizette's automatic pistol from her holster. He again shot the advancing soldiers down with no mercy and in rapid succession.

Everything suddenly became calm. He pulled Rizette closer into his arms and cradled her as a baby.

"Riz, Riz, don't leave me. Riz, please don't leave me."

The battle raged around them as always, but he couldn't hear or see anything but Rizette's dead stare into the sky. Tears began to fall onto her face as he wept and held her head close to his chest. He rocked back and forth as the pain inside became almost unbearable.

Several hours passed, and darkness settled on them before he finally found the strength to reach up and gently close her eyes with his fingers.

He looked down at her and wept again. During this time, he realized what mattered more than anything else. He realized how she had carried him along for the last month. All the times she had tried to encourage him and lift him up came rushing back to him.

Now he recalled how he reacted coldly as a child might rather than the partner and friend he should have been. As the night embraced him, exhaustion finally forced Oray to sleep while still cradling Rizette in his arms.

"Are you going to sleep all day?" When Oray heard this, he awoke still in the position of cradling someone in his arms. He looked up, and there sat Rizette.

A joyful noise erupted involuntarily from his mouth as he almost tackled her. He lay on her, kissing her face. She laughed and said, "Hey, hey!"

77

Now, tears fell on her face again, but this time they were tears of joy. She smiled and laughed a little as she tried to wipe his tears from her face and fend off some of his incessant kissing.

Once he had calmed down, they found an abandoned building to wait in for a few moments before moving forward again.

"I don't know. I felt something hit my chest, and there was some pain, then everything went black. I woke up by you, and that's when I woke you up."

Oray listened to his wife with an almost painful expression on his face.

"I'm so sorry for the way I've been acting, Riz. When I held you in my arms last night, I realized a lot of things. I realized you're the most important thing to me now. Nothing else matters."

She smiled a little when he said this. "Well, if I'd known all I had to do was die to get you back on track, I might have done it a long time ago."

Oray grimaced and looked down at the floor.

Realizing that probably wasn't a good thing to say right now, she got on her knees and moved over to him, then put her hands on his.

"I'm sorry." She then ran her fingers through his hair.

"It almost killed me seeing you that way. When I thought I might lose you forever, I realized what a lousy husband I've been lately. I thought of how you've been pulling me along and what a pathetic attitude I've had."

He paused and then looked into her eyes.

"I'm so sorry. I won't let you down again, I promise." He then looked back to the littered floor.

"I just felt like... this is all my fault. If I'd not taken that oath, maybe we wouldn't be here."

Rizette could no longer hold back a tear. As it rolled down her cheek, she lifted his head up to face her.

"Maybe, but maybe you would be drifting somewhere in here alone. Perhaps, if you hadn't taken the oath, I would be alone out there searching for you right now. I would rather be in here with you than out there without you. It's not your fault, Ray. And if this is all we have, then so be it. But I don't want to give up trying. I don't want to give up and then stumble onto something two years from now that may have helped get us out. If we die in here, I want to die knowing we tried everything possible to get out. If we lose hope, we will surely die in here. If we're alive and have each other, we still have hope."

Oray took her in his arms, and they held each other. He knew she was right, and he now knew what he had to do.

After a while, he got up and suggested they get something to eat and start new from today. Rizette now felt better than she had felt since the day they arrived. This was the Ray she needed. This was the husband she had missed so much.

They left the abandoned building and searched out the mobile ration dispenser. Oray began to move with a purpose and gleaned all the information Riz had gathered so far.

He felt ashamed when he realized how much work she'd already done as he'd soaked in self-despair. But he would make it up to her. He felt determined to make it up to her no matter what. That was his new purpose in life, and having an honorable purpose gave him renewed strength.

CHAPTER FIVE:

ALLIES

Oray now began to focus on any possible clue. Then, a week or so after Rizette had been shot, a thought came to him. They were walking forward with other soldiers when he slapped his hands together. Rizette looked at him, as did several other NLP soldiers walking past.

"I've got an idea."

"What?" Rizette asked with excitement.

Oray looked around just to make sure no one was close by.

"We've been moving forward all this time, simply trying to stay alive, right?"

She nodded, "Right."

"Well, this may not amount to anything, but here's my idea. We need to move with the safe zone to not get killed. We know that. And we need to find food and rest locations, but what if we begin to move to the left or right as we move forward. I mean, let's just say this is north." He pointed the direction the army was headed in. "So, let's start moving either northeast or northwest. We'll stay close enough to our known food dispersal locations to be safe until we locate another one, if we do locate another one."

Rizette thought about it a moment as the fighting ahead indicated they could stop a while. They walked over to a bombed-out building and sat on the remnants of the window ledge. Oray watched her giving his idea some thought as several tanks rolled noisily past.

"I think it's a great idea. If we can stay close enough to our current survival points but still locate new ones, maybe we can find something that will help us."

He now became even more enthusiastic with Rizette's vote of confidence.

"Right. We don't know what may be to the east and west of us. There may be nothing to help us, but we should make sure. At the very least, we may find a more hospitable location."

"But is there any chance the sequence will change if we leave a part of it. I mean, if we abandon this safe zone, can we be in danger of losing it? I don't want to get into a worse situation."

Oray thought about this.

"I don't know for certain. My guess would be this is a linear sequence with several randomized events interwoven. So, it may be possible by leaving an area, that area will change. But I'm hoping the foundational structure remains intact. By that, I mean we may leave this area, and it may change in appearance, but the safe zone will remain intact. My real hope is the safety zone runs all the way east and west. If this is the case, we can remain in that safe zone and explore as much area as possible while still inside it."

"I think we've got to try, Ray. We've got to search out anything that might help us out of here."

"All right, let's start tomorrow morning. We'll try to move with the safe zone, and if we locate a food distribution point, then we'll stay in that area until we contact another one." Oray glanced at Rizette, seeming to want an affirming gesture. She nodded as she stared out at the road.

"Yeah, we'll do that," she added after a few seconds.

The next morning, they began moving in the direction Oray now called northwest.

As they moved, the buildings became smaller, and after walking several miles, they moved into a housing area. The houses were similar in condition to the buildings. All were abandoned, and many were bombed out or burned. By asking some of the few other soldiers around, they located a ration dispersal vehicle and secured something to eat.

"How about if we stay in this area tonight?" he asked Rizette as she was eating. Since she'd been shot, he insisted one of them eat while the other stood guard.

She looked around at the houses. A few had children's toys or mangled swings in the yards.

"Okay, that sounds good. It'll be a change of pace at least."

Once they'd both eaten, the two began to cautiously search for a suitable place to spend the night. As the light gave way to darkness, they searched a house appearing only slightly battle-damaged.

In the twilight, Oray moved into the house first with his weapon held up in the ready position. Rizette moved behind him in an alert position as well.

She became a little distracted as she watched her husband. She'd never imagined him as a soldier. Yet, here he was, these many weeks later, a full-fledged, combat-ready soldier. She tried to regain her concentration. She didn't want to let him down if he needed her. She raised her weapon and tried to think as a soldier should.

"It's clear." Oray came back into the living room, where Rizette still stood with her weapon up and ready.

"You need to come and take a look at this."

She glanced at him with a puzzled expression while holstering her weapon.

As she stepped into the room and passed Oray, she saw something that almost made her cry. She put her hand up to her mouth and stared at the beautiful sight.

There, in the bedroom, was a queen-sized bed with the mattress still intact. Oray looked at her, and they both smiled. They'd not slept on an actual bed since their arrival in this harsh place.

Oray smiled slyly at his wife, and she knew well what he thought of. She also smiled and then nudged him.

"What? I didn't do anything."

They both laughed.

Later, Rizette wiped her naked body down with the small sanitary wipes distributed by the ration vehicle. The flashes of lights and sounds from the ever-present battle accompanied her in the bathroom of the abandoned house.

She looked at her face in the mirror. She ran her hand along her cheek and studied the person staring back at her as the battle flashes lit the room.

The face in the mirror appeared tired. It seemed difficult to believe now that this wasn't really her, that she was somewhere in a pod. She noticed the mirror wasn't flush against the wall. As she examined it further, she realized it could open, and in a cabinet, behind the mirror, all sorts of small medicine bottles and assorted items sat as if waiting for someone to come and use them.

Standing naked in the bathroom, Rizette examined the little medicine containers one by one. She would hold it until a large flash would light it up, and she could read what it was.

"Are you all right in there?"

The sound of her husband's voice brought her out of the strange trance she had drifted into.

"Yeah, I'm all right." She put a small bottle back into the cabinet and closed the mirror.

Then she walked into the bedroom with nothing on. Oray smiled as the flashes reflected on her naked body. He pulled a tattered blanket back in a manner to welcome her into the old bed.

They made love for the first time in a long time.

For over a week, they moved straight north and remained in this residential environment. Although the houses would change appearance, there would always seem to be at least one with very little battle damage.

In one of these less damaged houses, Oray sat on a broken-down couch and watched Rizette examine the pictures on the wall. His heart weighed heavy in his chest as she ran her fingers over the family pictures, seeming to yearn for what may never be.

"I think tomorrow we should move west again. We know now the environment changes. Maybe there's an end somewhere and an exit."

She didn't answer right away but seemed very interested in the picture of a man and woman holding two children in their laps. They all smiled as if everything were wonderful. Finally, she answered him in a soft voice.

"All right, let's do that."

As the days passed and they cautiously moved northwest, the residential area began to thin out. There were more open areas with sporadic houses and a few battered buildings with business signs on them.

Oray examined a dead NLP soldier in a black uniform. A vehicle with black paint and markings stood burning beside the road. He knelt and examined the soldier closer. He appeared to be an officer and had a set of powered binoculars around his neck.

Rizette held her weapon in a ready position and scanned the area as Oray pulled the binoculars from the dead soldier. He stood back up and with his weapon in the ready position, and they moved on, ever cautious of an attack.

That night they found a small building with remnants of cloth. The building had been some form of fabric store. Oray stared at the sky through holes in the roof. The flashes from bombs and fires would light the night, and then darkness would return briefly. Rizette lay with her head on his chest. She spoke softly.

"We're running out of time, aren't we?"

He didn't want to answer his wife's question but knew he must. After a brief pause, he spoke.

"The pods are designed to keep the body clean and hygienic. There is a basic muscle stimulating energy that flows through our bodies to keep the muscles from deteriorating into atrophy as quickly. Another maintenance aspect of the pod slowly moves our limbs enough to keep them from locking up. But, yes, we are slowly running out of time. After a year, I would suspect we would need physical therapy to regain our mechanical abilities. Within two years, I don't think we would be able to leave the pods without dying."

Rizette ran her hand back and forth across Oray's chest. She seemed happy that he'd told the truth rather than attempting to mislead her.

"I'm glad we're together. No matter what happens, I wouldn't want to live without you, whether we have two years or two months, just as long as we're together."

When she said this, a tear came to Oray's eye and trickled down the side of his head. He didn't bother to wipe the moisture from his skin. He didn't want Rizette to know about it. He held her tighter but couldn't say anything. He knew his voice would break if he tried to speak. They slowly fell asleep.

A few days later, the two hunkered down and examined something new to them.

"That's a communications center." Oray gazed through the binoculars at the large trailers with an armored vehicle hooked to the front to pull them. A screen of thin fabric stretched from poles over the top. Soldiers walked around the outside of these transporting units as other various military vehicles came and went. Oray handed the binoculars to Rizette.

"They're wearing gray uniforms, so they are on our side, right?" She studied the area as she asked this.

"Yeah, they're on our side. But from what little I know of military matters, I don't know that we should walk right up."

She handed the binoculars back to Oray. They sat at a distance from the open area with all the activity. The battle still raged, but here it seemed more distant. There were fewer planes and heliocraft overhead.

"If there are communications and database equipment in those vans, there may be some hope of doing something other than basic survival."

Rizette looked at him with a slight glimmer of hope when he said this.

"Are those systems connected to the main databases?" she asked in a low voice.

"Everything is connected to everything. But some systems are pretty much useless props. And then, there are systems that not only look like databases, but they are also functional databases. The designers tried to minimize confusing situations by incorporating databases in the virtual zone to actual hubs of functioning utilities. The question is, which one is that?"

Oray glanced through the binoculars again. Then he pulled them back down. "Let's try to stay close to this. We'll follow behind tomorrow, and if a ration dispenser comes close, we'll go to it to get rations. If the area is highly secured, we'll find out right away. Does that sound all right?" He glanced over at Rizette.

"Yeah, that sounds like a plan. At least we have something to work towards."

Oray smiled when she said this, and she smiled back. Right now, anything that would give her hope made him feel better.

The next morning, Oray and Rizette got up as early as they could and made their way in the pre-dusk light to where the communications caravan was set up. They felt relieved to find the caravan still there, though soldiers were preparing the unit to move. The thin fabric camouflage was being taken down, and the soldiers began to start their vehicles.

The two sat watching as the activity began to increase. Then, as daylight broke, a ration dispersal vehicle pulled into the area.

"There it is!" Oray became excited, and Rizette turned to see what he spoke of.

"Let's go." He stood up, then helped Rizette to her feet. They began to walk briskly towards the ration dispenser.

"Now, if we're allowed in, we'll hopefully be able to stay close," Oray said. He took Rizette's hand, and they approached the general area of the communications unit. They slowed down and scanned around for security.

"So far so good," Rizette said, somewhat under her breath as they walked up to the ration dispersal vehicle and got in line with the other soldiers.

Once they received their rations, they moved away from the vehicle.

"What next?" She glanced at Oray and began to open her food rations.

"Let's try to get a ride. I'd like to get a look inside those communications vans. Maybe we can stroll around by them first to make sure we don't get run off." Oray moved over towards the communications vans as he began eating his rations. Rizette followed along, scanning around as she also took small bites of food.

They approached the vans as soldiers quickly worked to prepare the vehicles for movement. Slowly, the two moved to the door of the rear vehicle. The door stood open, and as they gazed inside, soldiers could be seen in the well-lit interior. Two soldiers appeared to be eating, and one sat at a database working.

Oray scanned around quickly to make sure no one was watching them. He then began to move closer to the door.

"If I could get a better look at that equipment, maybe I could determine a little more about it." He seemed to be speaking to himself, but Rizette nodded in agreement. She followed behind as he crept up to the door, trying to be discreet while getting a look at the equipment.

Then, one of the men inside turned around rather quickly to throw his empty package into a wastebasket. When he did this, he looked straight at Oray and Rizette. Immediately, his face expressed surprise. Oray quickly turned around to face Rizette to cover the fact he was trying to look in. She, in turn, also acted as if they were talking or something.

As this happened and Rizette looked up at Oray's face, she saw a strange expression develop. First, he appeared a little frightened that he had been caught looking into the van. Then, his face changed into a puzzled look. After this, his eyes opened wide, and surprise came over his face.

"Wait a minute.... I've seen that guy before."

He quickly turned around to face the man in the van. The man inside the van still stood with an expression of shock when Oray turned back around.

Oray moved quickly towards the van with Rizette following behind in slight bewilderment.

"Vance?" Oray walked up to the man, who was speechless with surprise.

"You know my name?" he finally responded with a startled voice. This caused the other man inside the van to step up towards the door.

"How do you know my name?" Vance sounded very surprised by the development.

"I met you when I came to the diver department. I was still a class C diver. My name is Oray."

Vance now appeared to recall Oray. "Yeah, now I remember you. I thought you looked familiar when I saw you looking into the van."

Now the man behind Vance moved beside him to get a look at Oray.

"Oray, this is Layton. Do you remember him?"

"Hello, Layton. I heard about you, but you were gone before I came to the diver department."

He shook Layton's hand. He also seemed to be in a mild shock by the appearance of Oray and Rizette.

"I'm pleased to meet you, Oray."

Oray then turned to Rizette. "This is my wife, Rizette."

They both smiled and shook hands with her.

The four stood in silence for several long seconds as if none of them knew what to say. Finally, Vance spoke up.

"Well, we've been around these NLPs so long, Layton, we've completely forgotten our manners. You two come on in. We're about to move out anyway."

Vance stepped aside and motioned for them to come into the large communications van.

Oray and Rizette stepped up into the van. The lights were bright and clear. The van had control panels on both walls and numerous maps with assorted lit-up areas. As they came in the van and sat down, Oray and Rizette realized Vance and Layton's uniforms were clean. They also noticed both men were well-groomed. Oray rubbed the scruffy whiskers on his face and briefly wondered about this.

Vance and Layton sat down across from Oray and Rizette. Vance appeared to be the more talkative as he went right into a question session with Oray and Rizette.

"So, what are you two doing here?"

"We were about to ask you two the same thing." Oray laughed a little as he said this to Vance.

"So, you don't know anything?"

"Not much. We sure don't know who put us here. I have a few suspicions, but they're not very well-grounded. My theory is a faction of LPs and NLPs have taken control of an area in the virtual zone. This is the only thing I have to go on, and I don't have much there."

Vance and Layton appeared to consider this information.

"That's a possibility, I suppose. We seem to be at a loss for information as well. But listen, you two are probably in need of some rest and may wish to clean up. Let me show you two the living quarters before we start moving."

"Living quarters?" Rizette said and perked up when Vance said this.

"Yeah, the van next door is the living quarters. How long have you two been here?" Vance now seemed to notice the rough condition Oray and Rizette were in.

"Around two months," Oray replied.

"Oh, well, I suspect you two would like a shower. Those hygienic wipes from the ration kit don't go very far."

"A shower, are you serious?" Now Rizette began to beam. All three of the men laughed a little at this.

"Yes indeed, a shower. Come on. I'll show you everything, and we can talk later."

Vance then took them through a connection and a door to the van in front and showed them a shower room.

There were also clean bunk beds, and he directed one of the soldiers to clean their uniforms after giving them both some extra clothes that he and Layton had.

The van began to move a short time after Vance left. Oray and Rizette had some excitement as they tried to get cleaned up with the motion of the van.

But once they had a shower and sat down on the clean bunks, they laughed in each other's arms as the van swayed back and forth.

Oray felt so glad to hear Rizette's laugh again. And he tried to absorb the smiles and the little glimmer in her eye that had been absent for these many weeks.

Several hours went by as the van crept along at a slow but steady pace. Then it came to a stop. A knock came on the door that attached between the two vans. Oray opened the door, and Vance walked in.

"Well, you two seem to feel better. You look better anyway." He chuckled a little.

Oray rubbed his clean-shaven face. "That power razor does a much better job than those flimsy field razors."

When they all got sat down to talk again, Oray asked some questions he had for them.

"So, how did you guys get set up in this communication unit?"

They both chuckled a little, and Vance again began to speak first.

"Layton had already cornered this little piece of paradise when I showed up."

Layton smiled a little as Vance said this.

"I struggled like a mad man when I first got here. I thought I was going to go crazy. Have either of you been killed yet?"

Rizette raised her hand somewhat sheepishly.

"How many times have you been killed?"

"Just once," she replied softly.

"Consider yourself fortunate. I went headlong into the main battle, like an idiot, I might add. I got killed, as you'll do if you get too close to the battle. And then I got killed again during my effort to get away from the battle zone."

"Then, I tried to go the other way, and those officers at the rear."

Oray and Rizette both nodded in a manner indicating they knew which ones he spoke of.

"Yeah, they will shoot you if you try to go past them. I also found that out the hard way."

"So, you've traveled all the way north and all the way south?" Oray asked.

"North and south?" Vance asked, seeming a bit confused.

"Yeah, I guess. That's what we've been calling the area of the battle, north."

"I suppose that's as good as anything. Though I don't believe there's any real indication of which direction is which. The navigation equipment doesn't seem to be anchored to anything and can change from day to day. We may be going west one day, and then the next morning, we show to be going south."

Vance shifted his position slightly and continued.

"Here's the layout that Layton and I have put together so far. The combat zone is the city area. This is where most of the fighting occurs. If you've been here almost two months and spent much time in the city area, then I'm sure you've seen your fair share of combat.

"Then there's the residential area. That area has less combat but still receives random attacks and airstrikes. Finally, there's the rural area that we're in now. This is where the support stuff goes on. If you go farther that way, which you designated as west, you'll come across the officers' headquarters. That area is well guarded, and unless you're an officer, you can get shot there as well.

"If you go around the officers' headquarters, you'll enter into a city area again, and the cycle repeats, at least as far as we can tell."

"So, what is this place, and why would anyone want to come to such a horrible place?" Rizette asked, and Oray also wondered about.

Layton now spoke up.

"This seems to be an old-world military training sequence. You'll notice three sections, the combat section, the support troops section, and the officer section. We believe when this sequence was used in the old world, the soldiers would be dropped into the sequence related to the nature of their military service. So, if you were a combat soldier, you would be dropped into the combat zone. If you were an officer, you would be dropped into the officer zone. We feel this sequence was most likely used to orient troops to a combat environment."

As they spoke of this, the soldiers outside continued to set up the communications unit for the daily routine.

Layton continued.

"I found this unit the same as Vance, and possibly you, Oray; my original thoughts were of the databases and control panels. Once I realized there were no restrictions to being here, I simply stayed with the van. I believe our codes are of a high enough level that we don't get killed in the combat but not high enough for us to enter the officers' area. Our codes also seem to be undistinguished as far as either combat soldier or support soldier. I feel fairly confident this is the reason we can ride along with this support unit."

"What about him?" Oray pointed at the soldier sitting at a control panel. He'd not appeared to move since the time they first saw him. Vance chuckled a little when Oray asked about him.

"We call him 'Joe.' He's a very low-level NLP. All he does is sit and play with that fake control panel. He seems to have been written into the sequence simply to have someone in the communications van at all times."

Rizette examined the man at the control panel. "It seems creepy to have him there all the time."

"Yeah, at first it is. But you'll get used to him. He's not much for conversation, but then again, he never disagrees with you either." Everyone laughed when Vance said this.

Oray walked over to the largest control panel. "So, are these units of any value, or are they just for show as well?"

Vance and Layton moved over beside him as he looked the panels over.

"These are actually connected to the main database. If you notice, the streams of information are constantly changing. And we can pull an access point up to input information to the system. The problem is it requires a code to access the system. We've tried everything in the world we could think of. In fact, Layton and I spent several days in a row taking turns inputting random words to get into the system."

Oray sat down at the control panel. He examined the information feed in the hope of spotting something useful. After several minutes of examining the control panel, he asked.

"Is this the only control panel in the sequence?"

Layton and Vance had moved to where Rizette sat and was talking with her. Layton got up and walked over to Oray.

"We suspect there's a much better system at the officers' headquarters. But getting in there seems to be impossible."

Oray began to move the information feeds around with the touch of his finger. He wanted to get a feel for the system. Some of the feeds would move back to their original spot, and others would connect and assemble a new information feed.

"You see, the stats are all good. We can tell when enemy aircraft are headed in our direction. It also gives information regarding ration dispensers and other supply stats. But as far as information to get out of here, we've not found any yet."

After a few unsuccessful attempts of inputting an access code he was given for diver maintenance, Oray went back to Rizette's side. They talked about general subjects for the rest of the day and were all happier to have each other's companionship.

Although Oray didn't say anything to bring the good feeling down, he couldn't help but notice these two divers had been here much longer and had no success at getting out.

At least they seemed to be in a more comfortable environment, though. As he thought of this, he saw Rizette laugh at a story Vance was telling. He would be happy for now, and tomorrow, he would begin to work on a way out. He smiled when Rizette looked at him, and she smiled back. They must take every thin slice of happiness they could find now.

CHAPTER SIX:

AN OFFICERS' VIEW

The following day, Oray and Rizette noticed the routine following the same pattern as before. The soldiers began preparing the vans and other vehicles for movement early in the morning. The ration dispenser arrived at the same time.

The battle always seemed to be a little farther away than in the city or residential environment. Aircraft would fly over, and bombs would land close at times, but Vance and Layton said these always landed about the same distance away.

"There seems to be no way out."

Oray spoke to Vance as the two of them watched soldiers put the camouflage over the vans. Vance took a deep breath before answering.

"Layton and I have found nothing to indicate a way out. But then, we've had so little to work with. I'm sorry that you and Rizette are here, but you do bring more information, and that gives us a better chance. Every little bit of information we can put together may help at this point. We must remain hopeful."

After Vance said this, Rizette stepped out of the van and walked towards the ration dispenser. She smiled and waved at Oray and Vance. They waved back.

"I think I've given up hope for myself. But I'll never stop trying for Rizette."

Vance looked at Oray with compassion after he said this.

"Whatever you have that helps you move forward, Oray. You keep that close to you and apply that to our effort. If we ever give up, then we're certain to die here."

Oray chuckled a little when Vance said this. "Rizette said something very similar to that a while back."

"And she's right. We must always search for the way out, and in that process, we can remain hopeful."

That evening, they all sat in the communications van.

"This idea of a faction involving living personnel and non-living personnel; there might be something to this. It's interesting because Layton and I both were investigating some kind of 'creed' thing."

When Vance said this, Oray immediately sat up. This action caused Vance to stop talking for a second.

"You know something about this?" he asked Oray.

"This is the faction I was talking about. My assistant persisted in his efforts to get me involved with this thing he called the creed. I thought it was a glitch of some sort."

Layton now intervened.

"This is very interesting. I was approached by Commissioner Redstone several months before arriving here. He wanted me to investigate a potential channel in the lower level that provided complete access to the virtual zone. He said he had information concerning such a channel, and he wanted to shut down subversives trying to take control of the system."

Vance picked up on the conversation now.

"Then, after Layton became lost, the commissioner gave me the same assignment. He said this was all top secret as he didn't want to alert those seeking to oppose his leadership. Next thing I know, I'm in here."

Oray studied the new information from Layton and Vance.

"So, this may very well be a current faction rather than an old-world left over."

He then rubbed the side of his head and continued.

"I thought this may be something in the system from the old world. But if Commissioner Redstone was sending divers to investigate it, it seems to be a current threat. This could explain some things."

They all thought about this for a few seconds. Then, Rizette raised her hand meekly as if a student in school wishing to speak. The three men turned to her with a curious expression.

"This may not be anything, but if this is a rogue faction, why would they cause Oray to be a drifter after he joined them?"

When she said this, Layton and Vance both turned to Oray with an expression of shock.

"You joined this faction?" Vance spoke with obvious intrigue.

Oray sat back as if a secret had unexpectedly popped out.

"Well...I, uhm, I guess I may have joined it. But I thought it was a glitch. My assistant administered some type of crazy-sounding oath to the creed, and I took it thinking it would resolve the glitch."

Layton and Vance appeared to fall into a thought trance as they stared out at something into the air. Vance's face went blank for several seconds. Layton's head lowered until he seemed to be studying something on the floor while he tossed this new information around in his mind.

Finally, Vance spoke. "I don't know for certain what the meaning is, but that is a brilliant question, Rizette."

When he said this, Rizette smiled as if she'd been waiting for some remark concerning her question.

"Yeah, Riz, that is a great question," Oray said. Then they all sat in deep thought over what this could mean.

"Did you do anything that would make you an enemy of this group or whatever it is?" Layton asked.

"The only thing we did was to start asking around about the two of you. Actually, my assistant said three divers had become drifters."

Layton appeared to grimace a little when Oray said this, but he said nothing.

"So, two of us are here after trying to find out about this creed entity. You unwittingly took an oath that put you into this creed. And Rizette, it seems, is a victim of association. What does this add up to?" As Vance said this, he stood and walked to the door to gaze out.

"Did either of you find out anything about the group?" Oray asked.

Vance turned back around and looked at Layton, who appeared in no mood to answer the question. Once again, Vance spoke for both.

"We searched the lower-level databases for random access points. This is the procedure taught in diver school, so we followed the procedure; neither of us found anything of interest. But if this group can do this to us, then they could have easily known we were snooping around for information about them."

Oray perked up a little as if remembering something. "That reminds me. Part of this oath was about a 'creed station' and some other facilities or properties maybe. My assistant gave me some access keys."

Now, Vance quickly sat down in front of Oray, and Layton also moved closer to him.

"Access keys? What were they, words or numbers?" Vance asked with a sense of urgency now.

"They were words. But I don't really remember what the words were."

His face became strained as if painfully trying to recall the information.

"I just thought he had something wrong with him. I didn't pay much attention. Aghhh, I wish I'd paid more attention."

"But if Oray does remember the access words and we use them, won't that put us in the area of this group or faction?" Rizette asked with concern.

Vance quickly replied. "That may be. But other than this small fragment, we have nothing. If Oray can recall the access words, then maybe we can get somewhere or do something."

Oray continued to struggle. "There were two of them. Riley said one would give me basic access and the other would... do something, I can't remember. Both words started with an M, though, I'm almost sure."

"M, m, m, magic, monster, mortuary?" Vance began spitting out words that started with m.

"No, no, just let me think a minute." Oray rubbed his head with both hands now.

Layton seemed to understand. They were all getting tired.

"How about we get some rest, and maybe Oray can remember tomorrow."

Vance also realized they were all growing weary.

"Yeah, Layton's right. I think we've accomplished a lot today. We've got some leads, at least. We'll continue tomorrow."

Rizette and Oray nodded.

Oray stepped outside, and she followed him. It had grown dark, and Oray gazed out where the battle was still being fought, as it always was. He watched the flashes and listened to the sounds as if they were some forms of entertainment. Rizette eased up beside him and put her arm around him.

"I wish I'd paid more attention to that oath now," Oray spoke without turning from the sights and sounds of the battle.

"Don't get too worked up about it. Just relax, and it'll come back to you." Rizette wanted to calm him down. She now knew he may have the only thread of hope.

"Yeah, you're right, Riz. Maybe I'm still concerned about using the code if I do remember it. I mean, we have no idea who or what we're dealing with."

"I know. Let's just take this one step at a time. You try to remember the codes, and we'll see what happens after that."

He turned to Rizette, then took her in his arms and gave her a passionate kiss as the distant flashes of battle accented their loving embrace.

The next two days were spent trying to guess the words that started with an M. Then, after realizing they were going in circles, Layton suggested they begin a process of elimination.

Using the basic functions on the database control panel, they began assembling words in alphabetical order. As they put words together, one of them would say the words from lists. Oray would listen to them and consider each one. Though the process was a little frustrating, they all felt better to be doing something and to have a goal.

Days went by as the process slowly moved through the long list of words. Then something clicked.

Vance sat in front of Oray. As had been repeated many times, he would glance over at the display and then turn and say the word slowly and clearly to Oray.

"Monarch... Moniker..."

Oray suddenly sat up.

"Say that word again." He sounded excited. Vance again said the word slowly.

"Moniker..."

"That's close. It's something like that;" after he said this, Vance made some adjustments on the control panel.

"Good, that's good. We can adjust the word search to anything like this word." He then went to the door. Layton and Rizette were outside taking a break.

"We've got a lead." When Vance said this, they came into the van quickly.

Once they were close, the process developed much more rapidly. As the other two sat close by, Vance read off one word at a time until he said, "Monitor."

"That's it. I'm pretty sure that's one of the words." Oray exclaimed with enthusiasm. They all stared at him with keen interest.

"Are you sure?" Vance didn't want to get excited until he felt certain they had one of the words.

"I'm fairly sure that's the first access word. I was paying more attention during the first part of the oath. As Riley went on, though, I began to lose interest in what he was saying. But I'm almost certain that's the first word."

Everyone seemed to breathe out in relief that the recent days of effort were not in vain.

"Did Riley say how to use the access word?"

Oray turned to Vance. "He said something about it giving basic access. And there was something about an advisor. I began to fade from the conversation after that."

Vance became very serious. "We should proceed with caution from here. I think we need to think about our next move before we do anything else."

The rest nodded and agreed with this statement. As evening settled in, Oray had a strong sense of relief inside that at least he could remember one of the access words. He would worry about the other one later.

Rizette came over and put her hand on his shoulder as if to say, well done. He put his hand on her hand. Then, Vance slapped his leg before getting up. Layton also patted his other shoulder as he moved towards the living quarters van.

The next morning after eating, all four sat in the control van as it began to slowly move. Vance positioned himself at the main control panel and spoke up first as everyone appeared to be waiting for something to happen.

"Do we want to give it a try?" He examined the other three, who in turn looked back at him with some anxiety.

"What's the worst that could happen?" Rizette asked.

Vance replied in a flat tone.

"The worst? We could all be swallowed up by an instantaneous virtual fabric hole and be lost forever, or at least until we die."

Rizette grimaced a little at this. "Maybe I shouldn't have asked that."

"We've either got to try it or stay here till..." Oray stopped short as he knew none of them had any misconceptions about what 'till' meant.

Layton appeared tired, but he commented. "Yes, I think we have to try it."

"All right then, let's try it." Vance turned to the control panel after saying this and pulled up an input box.

"Here we go." He touched the screen, put "Monitor" in the box, then carefully touched the input button.

Nothing happened.

Now a deflated feeling seemed to settle over the four. The van continued to move slightly as it crept forward. Rizette grabbed the back of a chair to steady herself. No one seemed to know what to say as they all stared at the control panel.

After several seconds of silence, Vance said. "Maybe we need to use it with your ID. What's your ID number?"

"536," Oray replied.

Vance put that number with the access word. Again, nothing happened. He then tried "Oray 536 Monitor" in the box. Still, nothing happened. Now the feeling of disappointment set in even more.

They all sat down now and reflected on this new development. After a few moments of thought, Vance asked Oray.

"Did Riley say anything else as far as the access word? Is there anything you can remember that may be causing the word not to work?"

"No, he asked if I'd made a decision on the oath. I told him I would take it. Then he said we needed to... Hey, he made me stand in a C6 junction point as I took the oath. I thought this was odd and asked if it would cause a problem with the flow of information. He said that junction point was specifically designated for the use of administering the oath. He said something about the junction point recording my individual code information."

Vance sat back up from his slumping position as Oray said this.

"That means something. I believe if the system recorded your individual code, then maybe you must be the one to use the access word. Everything is connected, so the system may not recognize the access word because it's my code trying to use it. Here Oray, sit here and try to put the access key in."

Oray took a seat in front of the control panel. He pulled the input box up and put "Oray 536 Monitor" into the box. As soon as he hit the enter button, the entire control panel changed dramatically. Everything became clearer, brighter, and much more advanced than the drab military control panel that had been present before.

Vance stepped back in a mild shock, and the others, including Oray, uttered a sound of surprise and relief that something had finally happened.

On the display, they could read, "Welcome Oray 536. What do you wish to do?" They stared at this for a few seconds as if trying to believe what they were looking at.

Oray finally asked in a somewhat bewildered voice, "What do we wish to do?"

Vance just shook his head a little as if he didn't know. He then looked at Layton, who had stood up now, and stared at the display with a surprised expression.

"Ask about an exit, I suppose."

Oray nodded when Layton said this. He turned back to the panel and entered, "I need to find an exit from this sequence."

Immediately, the display answered. "There are no exits available within the facilities of this access code."

Everyone looked at each other now in the hopes one of them would know what this meant.

"Ask what facilities are available with this access code," Vance said.

Oray input the question, and the reply came quickly.

"Basic modifications of sequence parameters, basic adjustments to NLP actions, activation of the turnstile entry point." They looked over the three replies with keen interest.

"The turnstile thing, that was something Riley spoke of."

"That must be an exit from this sequence." Vance rubbed his chin as he said this. He then pointed to the display and said, "These two are in sequence activities. The turnstile must be the door out of here."

Layton now commented, "Out of here, but to where?"

When he said this, the others looked back at the screen with concern. They considered the vast number of possibilities.

Vance then said, "Ask for the location of the turnstile."

Oray typed the question in and entered it. The reply came instantly.

"Turnstile located outside current sequence parameters."

Everyone seemed to exhale a breath of disappointment. After a few seconds, Vance spoke up.

"Let's think about this. We're in, but exactly where we've gained access to may be something we should consider. We will obviously need to peruse the turnstile, but I think we shouldn't get in too big of a hurry. If the access code works after all these months, it should work tomorrow and the next day."

Everyone agreed with Vance. Later, they prepared themselves for bed. None slept well as they considered the possibilities.

Oray thought of the one thing that frightened him more than anything. What if he could leave but not the rest? He wouldn't leave

Rizette no matter what. The thought of this possible option now seemed worse than having no options. Finally, he slept lightly, as did the others.

The next day, the four followed their regular routine until after breakfast. Then they all assembled around the control panel. Oray sat gazing at the three options available to them.

"All right, we're fairly sure the actual exit isn't available to us with the first access code. If we can locate the 'turnstile,' we can most likely get out of here, but to where? I can't recall the second access word, and we're not sure what to do with it if I could. So, what can we do with what we have available to help us?"

They all studied the options on the display for a few minutes, and then Vance seemed to think of something.

"How about this? It sounds like we can change our situation in this sequence, right?"

Oray nodded as if he agreed but wasn't sure where Vance was going with this.

"How about we try to get into the officers' headquarters, and maybe there will be better equipment to work with."

When Vance said this, Oray smiled, and then the others smiled.

"I believe that idea has some potential," Oray said and, after a brief pause, continued. "We can always come back?"

"Sure, we can. If there's nothing to help us at the officers' headquarters, we just come back here and work from the van."

Once Vance had said this, Oray turned back to the control panel and positioned himself to work. Then he seemed unsure of what to do.

"So, do we just want to receive access to the headquarters?"

Vance replied.

"I think if we're all officers, we could access everything. Can you adjust the sequence so that we're mid-level officers or something?"

"Yeah, the system should let me do that. But will we be put into action or anything?"

Vance thought about his question for a few seconds.

"I don't think so. We seem to be in a neutral state here, only bound by the framework of the sequence. We can't cross the borderlines of the sequence, but we don't seem to have any actual functions. I suspect if we're officers, the same will hold true. If we are put to work, you can just adjust the sequence again."

Oray nodded in confirmation of Vance's assessment and went to work at the control panel.

After he finished entering the information, nothing happened.

They all looked at each other with puzzled expressions, and then Layton commented.

"We may need to sleep first. I've noticed major adjustments always seem to go into effect after we sleep."

"That's probably right. Every time I got killed, I would wake up the following morning, no matter what time of day I got killed. It appears the night is used for major adjustments inside the sequence."

The others agreed with Vance's assessment, and Oray stated this was also the case when Rizette was killed.

For the rest of the day, they continued to discuss any possible ways the new development could assist them.

The following morning, Oray woke up and stared at an unfamiliar ceiling overhead. As he sat up and looked around, he realized he was in what appeared to be a battle-damaged, abandoned mansion. The room was large and obviously part of a massive house. Yet, there was a large shell hole in the wall, and pictures on the walls hung at odd angles.

He stood up and noticed the bed was large and ornate. The blankets were satin or some similar expensive material.

Oray then walked cautiously over to the large hole in the wall and gazed out. This revealed that his room was on the second story. As he looked down, he observed several staff vehicles parked in front of the mansion. Uniformed drivers lingered around the cars, seeming to be in a perpetual state of readiness for any officer needing to go somewhere.

When he moved to the bedroom door, he passed a mirror and became aware that he wore pajamas. He stopped and examined himself in the mirror. They were of a plain, military type, but still, he chuckled at the fact as he looked them over.

Walking into the hall of the mansion, he tried to find Rizette. As he began to stroll up the spacious hall, a door opened, and out walked Rizette. She also wore plain military pajamas. When she saw Oray in his sleeping wear, she immediately laughed.

"Yeah, I know. Really funny, right?" He pulled the sides of the drab pajamas out a little as if to enhance the humorous view for his wife. From around the corner came Vance, also dressed in the drab pajamas.

"Something obviously worked," he said when he saw Oray and Rizette. "Has anyone seen Layton?"

"I just go up myself," Oray replied.

"I haven't seen him. Maybe he's already downstairs," Rizette said.

"That could be. Let's get dressed and see if we can find him." Vance then turned back towards his room.

Back inside his room, Oray scanned around and found a clean, pressed uniform draped across a plush chair that had several bullet holes through it. He put the uniform on and met the other three in the hallway. They also wore clean and pressed officers' uniforms.

Oray chuckled a little at the sight of his wife's very distinguished appearance. In turn, she slapped his arm as she came up to him and said, "You better watch it, mister."

"Yeah, I'm going to watch it, all right." He smiled and winked at her. She smiled back, and they trotted down the elegant staircase.

"I know one thing for certain. I'm going to do some more adjustments to the sequence. I'm not going to wake up in that massive bed again without you."

She laughed at this just as they came to a huge, open room. In the middle sat a large table with breakfast prepared. Several soldiers stood by wearing white aprons, and as they came closer, the soldiers pulled plush dining chairs out for the three to sit in.

"Now, this is more like it," Vance said as they sat down. Then, more officers began to arrive and sat down at the table. Soon, these officers were eating and talking about an offensive, as well as other tactical subjects. The soldiers who wore white aprons and clean uniforms brought breakfast around the table, and all three began to eat. Still, there was no sign of Layton.

Then, about halfway through breakfast, they saw Layton trotting down the stairs in the same drab pajamas the others woke up in.

"Hey, I've been looking all over for you three."

Vance raised his coffee cup as he, Oray, and Rizette all began to laugh.

"Welcome to the officers' club, Layton."

Layton stood looking over the large table of food, and then he smiled and chuckled a little as if realizing, at the very least, life had just gotten a little better.

The NLP officers paid little attention to the four new officers. If spoken to, the NLPs would discuss matters casually, but the conversation always moved to the battle, the soldiers, or even the equipment.

Every day they would move forward to a new location. These locations would generally be an abandoned house or building. But the new accommodations would always be much nicer than anything else around. Even the few occasions spent in tents were more elaborate and comfortable than the communications van.

The three divers went to work right away with the new and much more extensive databases of the officers' headquarters.

"Well, you got anything yet?" Vance hovered over Oray's shoulder as he worked with the elaborate control panel.

"No, it's the same thing. We've got to do something else. There's nothing in the system referring to an 'advisor.' I've also been through every word starting with M twice, at least. I don't understand why I can't find the second access word."

Oray then spun around in his chair and stood up.

"What's left? We've been here over a month and still can't find anything to move us forward."

He walked to the window of the large house they were headquartered in. He stared out and then said in a lower voice.

"Layton is fading. Soon we'll all be fading as well and unable to think straight."

Vance looked down at the floor when Oray said this.

"He's been fading for months now. I think he knows it, but we just never talk about it."

"Well, you'll be next, Vance. I need your help for any chance of us to get out of here. We need Layton as well, but it seems he's losing his facilities much faster now."

"He's done his part. We would never be as far as we are now without him."

"I know that. I'm just frustrated. The longer we remain in the virtual zone, the less we'll be able to function at the necessary levels to find a solution. What can we do? There must be something we can do."

"How about we all go for a ride?" Rizette stood in the doorway, leaning on the frame. They'd not seen her, and she apparently heard the entire conversation.

"How long have you been there, Riz?"

"Long enough; I think we all need to get away from the problem for a while. We have staff cars outside, ready to go, and we've never used them for any reason other than moving forward every day. I think we should just go ride around a while and stop banging our heads against the virtual walls."

The two men glanced at each other and then back to Rizette.

"Sounds good to me. What do you think, Oray?"

"I like it. We shouldn't let a good staff car sit idle for too long now, should we?"

The other two laughed a bit, and Rizette smiled slyly. "I'll go find Layton."

As the four walked down the steps of the large battle-damaged mansion, several soldiers stood up from sitting on the steps and saluted them. All four gave a casual salute back, having by now become accustomed to it.

Noticing the four officers heading his way, a driver jumped up and immediately saluted them. They again gave a quick return salute.

"We need you to drive us around, corporal."

The soldier appeared puzzled when Vance said this.

"Drive you around... where sir?"

"Just drive us around, anywhere that we won't get shot or bombed." As Vance said this, the others climbed into the large staff vehicle.

"Uhmm, ah...yes sir. I'll drive you around then."

The driver got in, and they were soon cruising along the war-ravaged roads with no destination in mind.

As the air flowed into the vehicle and the broken buildings and bombed-out tanks passed, Oray realized Rizette had a great idea. The main battle always seemed to be a little farther away since they had become officers. They seldom saw a living soldier in the black uniform anymore. And although the old mansions and buildings they moved to every day always had damage, they never witnessed the actual fighting that caused it.

He relaxed as they drove around. The military vehicles and soldiers all on their way to the battlefront became a blur as he laid his head back and slowly closed his eyes. Yes, Rizette had a great idea. They just needed to get away from everything for a while.

"Wait, stop the car!"

The vehicle stopped as Vance had ordered. Oray raised his head quickly, briefly wondering how long he'd dozed off.

"What is that?"

The driver looked at the long building with the large red crosses on it.

"That, sir? That's the medical facility," the driver replied, seeming puzzled that an officer would ask him such a question.

Oray sat up now and looked at what Vance spoke of. The long, wide building appeared to be made of aluminum sections that could be taken down and put back together.

Several medical personnel worked around the building, and a few soldiers who appeared to only have minor wounds sat outside as well.

As they sat and examined the facility, a drab-gray ambulance with a faded, red cross pulled up and offloaded wounded soldiers.

"I've never seen this before. Have you ever seen this, Layton?"

Layton shook his head to indicate he hadn't. All four began climbing out of the staff vehicle with obvious curiosity.

"This area must only be accessible from the officer zone," Oray said as he returned the salute of a passing soldier.

When they entered the medical building and began walking past the wounded soldiers, a nurse approached them.

"May I help you?"

"We're...just inspecting the facility, nurse."

"Yes, sir. If you need anything, just let me know." As the nurse began to walk away, Vance thought of something else.

"Uhmm... Nurse, I would like to ask you a question." The nurse turned and stepped back to the four officers.

"Yes, sir?"

"Well, I wondered, if you know of anything about an 'advisor' in this facility?"

"Advisor, well, I guess that would be Captain Lenore. He's our psychological therapist."

When the nurse said this, all four immediately perked up and looked at each other with a newfound enthusiasm.

111

"Where could we find Captain Lenore?"

"He would be in the office at the end. It's the one on the right, sir." The nurse pointed to the far end of the building.

"Thank you, nurse." As soon as Vance said this, they all began walking briskly past the wounded soldiers towards the far end of the building.

At the end and on the right, they found a small office with a single desk and a large cabinet inside. Behind the desk sat a small man examining papers. He wore glasses, and as they knocked lightly on the door and stepped into his office, he appeared a bit startled.

"May I help you?"

With all four inside the small office, there wasn't much room. They stood in front of the desk as the captain gazed up apprehensively. Vance looked at Oray expectantly. Oray nodded in confirmation of what he knew Vance was thinking.

"Are you an advisor?" Oray asked without emotion.

"Well, yes, I suppose you could call me that. Why do you ask?"

"I'm Oray 536. I wish to access Monitor."

When Oray said this, Captain Lenore's face went blank. He stood slowly and mechanically. He took a step over to the large cabinet and opened the door. It immediately became a light doorway.

All four expressed shock as this had transpired suddenly and quite unexpectedly. They looked at each other as the bright light from the doorway lit their stunned faces.

"So, are we going?" Layton finally asked as the others stood motionless. Oray looked at Layton.

"I guess we should. Can anyone think of a reason we shouldn't go now?" They stood and considered Oray's question for a few seconds. Then Vance replied.

"We've used the database for everything possible. We can't reveal the second access word from the database. I can't think of any other reason we would need to stay. Maybe there's an exit somewhere through this doorway, or we find something to help us in another sequence."

They all seemed to agree with Vance's assessment of the situation.

"All right then, if we're all in agreement, let's go then."

Rizette took a deep breath when Oray said this, and the other two nodded. Oray then stepped through the doorway.

Immediately, after Oray stepped through the doorway, the light went out, and only the empty cabinet could be seen.

"NOOO...!" Rizette screamed and ran to the empty cabinet. "Oray...!"

She began to cry and fell to the ground in front of the cabinet. Suddenly, she realized how Oray must have felt when she got shot. How could she survive without him?

The other two men awkwardly moved to help her up.

"No...." She wept aloud as they picked her up from the floor. "Oray, don't leave me..."

Rizette's tears flowed down her cheeks like a child. She didn't care who saw her cry. She realized she couldn't go on without her husband. Oray was what held her together, and she began falling apart immediately with the thought of losing him.

Oray found himself in a large circular room. He took a step forward to make way for the others. Everything gleamed white, and the room was well lit. All around the room were doors with only a knob on them. He glanced around and guessed there were twenty doors at least.

"This must be the turnstile," he said as if the others were behind him. He then looked back and realized the door was closed. "No, no, no!"

His previous fears now suddenly came rushing back. He grabbed the doorknob and turned it as he also pulled. The door came open with a burst of light, and he stepped quickly through.

Suddenly, the captain's office lit up, and out of the cabinet stepped Oray. Then as he stepped through the door, it closed again, and the room appeared dark after the bright light of the doorway went out.

"Oray!" Rizette almost shouted through her tears. She jumped up and grabbed him in an embrace and held him tight. He held her and tried to contain the tears that welled up in his own eyes.

"Maybe we should think about this a bit more," Vance said solemnly.

They walked back through the medical facility as Oray held Rizette, who continued to weep from the fright she'd received.

All the way back to headquarters, Rizette held her arms tightly around her husband. She only regained her composure as they pulled up to the large house they'd left from earlier.

Later, at the large dining table, the four sat in silence as the soldiers served the food. While the other officers spoke to each other about the battle situation, Oray glanced over at Rizette, who picked at her food more than eating it. He wondered what they could do now. He wouldn't leave her. The scare he had earlier lingered inside him as a sour taste, difficult to wash from his mouth.

The following day, Vance, Oray, and Layton talked as the staff vehicle moved them forward again.

Rizette sat quietly staring out the window as she still seemed to be recovering from the previous day's scare.

"It must have been the turnstile. There were at least twenty doors all around the circular room. I remember now, Riley said I would need to go through the turnstile and to another sequence to use the second access word."

"It has to be the turnstile then," Vance replied.

Layton appeared to be in thought about the turn of events.

"We'll need to try again. It's our only option."

When Vance said this, Rizette turned and looked at the three men with obvious apprehension. She then turned back to the window without saying anything.

114

Oray noticed this and felt his heart fall a bit. He knew what she thought because he thought the same thing. He gazed down at the floor of the car and tried to think of anything that could improve the outlook.

The staff vehicle pulled up to a damaged hotel. Then, something did come to him.

"How about this? The door closes when I go through, right?"

Now Rizette turned again to listen.

"What if the three of you go through first? That way, if it doesn't work, then I won't go through, but if it does, I can follow you and go through as I did before."

This caused an immediate effect on Rizette. She sat up a little and began to show more interest in the conversation. The driver opened the door, and all four began to exit the vehicle.

As they walked into the lavish but obviously damaged and abandoned hotel, Vance replied.

"That's a great idea, less risk as far as I can see. I think we should try it tomorrow if everyone agrees."

Later, in their room, Oray knew he needed to talk with Rizette. She sat on one of the plush chairs after dinner and said nothing. Oray came and sat beside her.

"Are you worried about tomorrow?"

She turned to him with sadness in her eyes. After a few seconds of thought, she replied.

"I think I finally realized how critical our situation is when I thought I'd lost you. Even though I didn't lose you then, I know now that we may lose each other somewhere else. If we do make it to another sequence, our codes may be different from here, right?"

Oray now considered what had been bothering her. She was right. If they did make it to another sequence, their codes could possibly be changed. If one of them were to be killed, he or she might not be restored to the sequence as before. He really didn't know where they could end up or how dangerous the situation might be.

"You're right. We don't know. But I can tell you this. We don't know that we can't make it out of here together and have a real life once we do make it out. We don't know unless we try. We only fail when we give up hope. You're the one who taught me that."

Rizette smiled a little when he said this. Then she turned away, so he wouldn't see the tears roll down her cheeks.

"I can't go on without you." When she said this, Oray could tell she was crying. He put his arm around her, and she turned and put her head onto his chest as he embraced her.

She began to weep even more as he held her. She felt bad that she was being weak. She wanted to be a stable source of strength for Oray, but after the frightening experience, she realized how much she needed him. He held her until she calmed down again. She didn't see the tear softly escape from his eye, and he did everything he could to hide it from her. He helped her to bed, and they slept in each other's arms.

The next morning after breakfast, the four once again went to the waiting staff car. Again, they saluted soldiers on the way. This time, they instructed the driver to take them directly to the medical facility. This time, they found the building being put together and some wounded inside the completed part and others in beds outside. Medical personnel attended to these wounded and worked around the soldiers putting the building together.

The four moved into the large opening of the building. No wall or door stood on the end of the building yet. They moved past the busy soldiers and nurses.

When they reached Captain Lenore's office, he could be seen putting items up and unpacking from the recent move.

"Captain Lenore?"

The captain stopped working when Oray said this.

"Yes?"

"Oray 536, I wish to access Monitor."

Again, the captain's face went blank. Once again, he moved over to the cabinet in a mechanical motion and opened the door. The bright, light door again lit up the room.

Oray took a deep breath as he stared at the entrance. "Let's try to hold onto each other as we go through, and I'll go last."

The others nodded, and Layton seemed to volunteer to be the first as he stepped close to the door and hooked his arm together with Vance's. Rizette took Vance's other arm and then latched onto Oray around his waist and held him as if they were about to walk off a cliff together.

"All right, let's go," Oray said.

Layton moved into the bright light and disappeared, then Vance and finally Rizette and Oray. As soon as Oray had gone through the door, it disappeared, and only a door identical to the others in the turnstile stood where it was.

CHAPTER SEVEN:

GETTING OUT OF DODGE

All four no longer wore their officer uniforms but now wore the light gray overalls like Riley always wore.

After months of the constant sounds of battle, the silence of the turnstile felt almost overwhelming. Everything was white and spotless. Light seemed to come from everywhere and yet nowhere, all at the same time.

They all stood gazing around the large open area. The circular-shaped room had a multitude of doors. Rizette continued to cling to Oray, as if the danger of losing him might still be present.

Oray thought he should say something before they stepped away from the door they'd just come through.

"I think we need to consider a few things before we lose track of this door." His voice didn't carry far in the round room, but the other two turned and stood before him and Rizette.

"We have no idea where these other doors will take us. Even if we do make it to this 'station' or whatever it is, we may find ourselves in the middle of a hostile faction. Once we cross into another virtual sequence, our code levels may change. If we get killed in a different sequence, we may not be restored. I think we should take careful consideration of these things before we move from this point."

Rizette continued to hold her husband as a child might hold her father. Vance and Layton stood in obvious thought of the situation at hand.

Then Vance spoke.

"It seems certain that once we go through another door, we can only find the turnstile again by locating another advisor. Who knows how difficult that may be? But we may also be in a better situation than the one we're leaving."

Layton then noted in a soft voice, "Or we could be in a worse situation."

Vance continued.

"Yes, that's true. From what we now know, there seem to be more sequences available than what we were ever aware of."

After he said this, they all thought again in silence. Then Vance continued.

"I think we've got to keep moving. We've gone this far, and that's a lot farther than Layton and I thought we could go. We don't know that we'll make it out, but we don't know that we won't either."

Again, they considered this. Then Oray spoke up.

"I agree. If we don't try, we'll always wonder if we could have made it out. I think Vance is right. We don't know that we won't be in a better situation, and we don't know how far we can go unless we keep moving forward."

He glanced down at Rizette, who had her head on his shoulder. She realized he wanted her input, and she nodded her head to confirm she stood with him in whatever decision he made, so after this, Oray continued.

"We'll keep going."

Then Vance said, "I'll keep going."

Finally, Layton nodded and said, "I'll keep going as well."

Oray took Rizette's hand. They moved away from the door and towards the middle of the room.

"I don't see anything to give us a clue as to which door we should take," Vance said.

They all continued to examine the doors for anything to distinguish one from the other.

"I don't think there's any way to determine which would be better or worse. How about we just take the one you're facing, Oray?" After Vance suggested this, Oray looked straight ahead at the door he faced.

"I suppose that method of picking is as good as any."

He then moved to the door and opened it. The bright light streamed in. "Are we ready?" Layton again took Vance's arm, and Rizette took Vance's other arm as well as Oray's arm. They proceeded one by one through the door.

When Oray passed through the light door, it closed behind him.

A strong, pungent odor caused him and the others to flinch in shock before any other senses could help them get oriented.

"Aghh, I know this smell. It's got to be horses." Rizette put her hand to her face.

Oray looked around and tried to cover his nose as well. They all stood in a large building, and on both sides were stalls. Inside the stalls were horses. Oray had never actually been this close to a horse, much less smelled one.

"I didn't know they smelled this bad," he said through his muffled mouth.

"Oh yeah, the smell never changes. But why are there so many?" Rizette also spoke through a hand-covered mouth.

Then they began to look at each other.

The first surprise was Rizette wearing a dress that went all the way to her ankles. There seemed to be nothing spectacular about the blue dress other than Rizette wearing it. She still appeared to be struggling with the odor of the horses when the three men noticed her, one by one.

As each man noticed Rizette in the strange apparel, he stepped back and examined her with obvious curiosity. When all three stood around her expressing the same strange stare, Rizette finally realized they were looking at her.

"What?" she asked, still holding her hand over her mouth and nose. None of the men said anything but continued to look at the odd sight of Rizette in the long dress. Then, she looked down and realized what she wore.

"What is this? Oh, no way, aagghhh. This is wrong, wrong. What is this, this...thing on me?"

She pulled the dress up and exposed her bare legs. "What is this?"

Now she moved around as if she were in a trap.

"I can't believe this! Am I supposed to wear this? And those stinking horses, ahhgg, this is awful." She put her hand on her nose again. "What is this place?"

As she struggled to come to terms with her apparel, the men examined the drab pants and coarse threaded shirts they wore. Layton also wore an odd hat that appeared to have been past its prime years ago.

Finally getting over the shock of his uncomfortable clothing and the sight of Rizette in a dress, Oray spoke.

"I don't know for certain, but I think it must be an ancient history sequence. These clothes and the horses, everything points to ancient history."

Vance nodded in agreement. "I think you're right. But let's get out of here. The smell must surely be better outside." He then led the way out the large door and into the sunshine.

Immediately, a loud and fast-moving wagon pulled by horses almost ran the four of them over. They stepped back and tried to breathe as the dust floated around their faces.

Vance moved along the side of the street after this. The others followed along cautiously behind him. Rizette continued to have trouble walking in the long dress and odd shoes with high heels. Oray held her arm to keep her from falling.

As soon as they reached what appeared to be a wooden walkway, a mass of animals began to move past them with much noise and commotion. The animals had horns, and all made an odd "moo" sound. Again, the four put their hands to their noses as the smell repulsed their senses.

"Agghh," Rizette complained aloud again as she stumbled onto the wooden walkway, with one hand holding her dress up almost to her knees and the other covering her nose.

"Is there no place around here that doesn't smell bad?"

The huge mooing animals with horns crowded almost onto the wooden walkway as the four struggled to maneuver out of their way.

Eventually, the mass of animals passed by, and this strange sight was accented by the vision of men riding horses and obviously herding the animals down the street. They yelled and whistled along, swinging their hats about in their hands occasionally.

Several of these men caught sight of Rizette on the walkway. They waved at her as she stood holding her dress up to her knees with one hand and the other handheld over her mouth.

Vance noticed this, and after the third one waved at her, he had to comment on the strange occurrence.

"They act like they know you, Rizette."

After he said this, the other two men also turned to her as if expecting an answer to the odd incident.

She continued to hold her hand in front of her face to avoid the smell, but with a puzzled expression, looked at all three, one by one.

"I don't know any of them. How would I possibly know any of them? I don't know why they're all looking at me."

Then, after saying this, she reached down and took a better hold on the uncomfortable dress. She then pulled it higher to get it away from her legs. This put it up over her knees.

A few seconds later, a man on a horse riding by saw her and pulled his horse to a stop in the street. He tipped his hat to her.

"Hello there, little lady. How're you this fine day?"

Rizette sort of waved with the hand she was using to cover her nose. Then, the man kicked the haunches of his horse and yelled out in apparent joy as the horse ran towards the other men and odd animals.

Now, Oray turned to his wife with a questioning expression on his face. Rizette still had her hand over her nose. She shrugged her shoulders and, grimacing a bit, shook her head to indicate she also didn't understand why the men were paying so much attention to her.

"Ray, I have no idea why these men keep acting like they know me. Can we just go? This ridiculous thing I'm wearing is hot." Again, she pulled her dress higher in an effort to cool her legs.

Oray shook his head a little and appeared frustrated. They turned and walked down the walkway again, with Rizette still holding the front of her dress high above her knees.

A man approached them and seemed to be having some trouble walking.

"Well, hellooo there, missus.... I'm mighty pleased to see yaa this here fine mornin'...."

The man seemed to only see Rizette as they approached him on the wooden walkway. He tipped his worn-out hat and looked a little disoriented as he spoke.

In turn, she expressed more aggravation that men were making such a fuss over her, particularly in front of her husband. The man looked her up and down and seemed to gaze down at her legs more than once.

"Do you know me?" Rizette had anger in her voice but continued to hold her dress up as if it were completely normal, seeming unaware of the man's continued attention to her exposed legs.

"I'm not sure.... Maybes I do.... We can go have a drink to stir my memory Ms.... I might recall knowing you after a drink...."

After saying this, he took hold of a support beam to catch himself from falling.

"I will not have—"

Before Rizette could finish her angry words, Vance took her arm and pulled her back.

"Wait a minute." He then turned to the man, who still held onto the beam.

"She'll be right with you."

"What are you doing, Vance? Just let me punch this guy, would you?" Rizette was obviously angered by the situation.

Oray and Layton both moved closer to find out what Vance had in mind.

"Listen, I remember hearing about potions and tonics for health issues during this ancient period. Did you hear him say this 'drink' would help him remember you?"

She glanced past Vance to look at the man.

"Yeah, but I'm not going anywhere with that guy. In fact, I have a strong urge to knock him out."

Her months in the harsh combat sequence became apparent to the men. Oray smiled slightly when she said this.

"No, no. I don't expect you to go anywhere with him. Just try to find out what the drink is that helps him remember stuff. Maybe we can get some, and it will help Oray remember the creed information."

After saying this in a low voice, they all glanced back at the man to make sure he was still there. He stood leaning against the beam and appeared to be staring at Rizette's legs with great interest.

"Well, all right, I guess I can do that." She pulled the dress up a little higher to help her walk and then stumbled, in the unfamiliar shoes, back to the man.

"Uhmm, hello again.... You ahh, you said something about a potion to help you remember me?" When she said this, the man looked up at her strangely.

"I did? I don't remember that. I think I need a drink."

"Yes, that's what I mean. You said there's a drink to help you remember stuff?" She gazed at the man expectantly.

"Well...yes, I drink to remember stuff and forget stuff. Drinking always helps me with my memory...." His attention then seemed to drift back down to her legs.

"So, what is this 'drink' you speak of?" She watched him with anticipation for an answer.

His head bobbed a little as he pulled his eyes from Rizette's lifted dress.

"Well, I don't know about you lil' lady, But I jus drink good ole whiskey.... That does the trick for mezz every time...."

"Whiskey?" she asked with a confirming tone.

"Yes, ma'am, whiskey."

Rizette turned to the others now, and they all seemed to be repeating the word silently to memorize it.

"Where... uhhm, could we get some of this 'whiskey,' if we wanted some?"

The man's head again bobbled a little as he thought about Rizette's question.

"Where do you get whiskey? I get mine at the saloon over there." He pointed to a building across the dirt street.

"All right. That's great, uhmm. Well, thank you, sir."

"You want to go have some whiskey with me, lil lady?" His eyes again slowly fell towards her exposed legs.

"Maybe later. I'm kinda busy right now," she then smiled politely at him.

"All right, maybe later," he then half walked, and half stumbled away as the four turned to each other to discuss the new information.

"If this potion actually helps you remember things, it may be good we landed in this sequence," Vance said.

"I've heard these ancient potions had side effects. That's the reason they quit making them. I don't want Oray taking anything that could hurt him." Rizette still sounded agitated.

Oray turned to his wife. "Listen, Riz, surely one dose can't be that bad. I mean, that guy seems to drink a lot of this 'whiskey stuff,' and he looked..." Oray thought for a second. "Well, he looked...sort of normal. But if one dose can help me remember, I'll take a chance."

She glanced at Oray. All three men now looked at her as if awaiting confirmation of their plan. She pulled her dress up a little more and waved her hand to cool her legs off as she thought about it. Finally, she spoke softly.

"I suppose so. I am ready to get out of this place. It smells bad, and it's dirty. Not to mention this...thing I'm wearing is hot and uncomfortable. And these boots or whatever they are, they're killing my feet." Rizette lifted her shoe and turned it a little to show the others the strange footwear.

"All right then, let's look into this whiskey stuff. If I can remember the other access word, maybe we can get to an exit before dark." When Oray said this, the others nodded in agreement, and they turned their attention to the saloon across the street.

Rizette held her dress up high off her legs with one hand, and holding onto Oray with the other, they made their way across the street.

As they walked through two swinging doors and into the saloon, they found themselves in front of several tables in a large open area. At one of these tables, a man sat with several women dressed in flashy outfits. Though they were like the one Rizette wore, these were more colorful, and the length was much higher, exposing the women's legs.

"Now why can't I have something like they're wearing? I hate this long heavy thing."

Oray simply nodded a little as she whispered this to him.

The women and man looked at the four of them with keen interest as they moved on into the building.

Past the open area was a small stage. To the right of the open area was a long table that stood almost chest high. Behind this long table was a large mirror and many bottles and glasses. A man with a long mustache stood behind it also. He looked at the four of them with the same interest as the two women and the man at the table.

The man at the table then stood up as they walked past him. When they reached the long table, music began to play. Oray glanced back and noticed the man at the table now sitting at some type of machine, striking his fingers onto white and black buttons that caused the sound of the music.

"Can I help you?" the man at the long table asked as he wiped it with a cloth.

"We would like some of the potion 'whiskey,'" Vance replied with a tone of reservation.

The man behind the counter looked at Vance a bit oddly and then turned. He glanced at the bottles and pulled a large one from a shelf and sat it in front of them. Vance reached up to take the bottle.

"That'll be two bits," the man behind to counter said quickly before Vance ever touched the bottle.

"Two...bits?" Vance and the others appeared somewhat confused by this. The man behind the counter reached up and pulled the bottle back a little.

"Two bits; you all aren't from around here, are you?"

Now, the four became a little nervous, but all stood firm and showed no outward concern.

A woman who looked to be fifty-something walked behind the long table and seemed interested in the activity.

"What's wrong, John?"

The man behind the counter replied to the woman with obvious respect.

"These people want whiskey but don't appear to have any money, Miss Lilly."

When John told her this, Miss Lilly examined the four of them for a second.

"You don't have any money?"

"We don't have any money. But we're willing to work if there's something we can do to earn some 'bits.'" Vance again tried to sound as if he knew what he spoke of.

Miss Lilly looked at them with a great deal of suspicion. She then walked around from behind the long table. As she came to where they stood, the four turned to face her.

She appeared to take extra notice of Rizette, who stood holding her dress up above her knees. She studied her exposed legs carefully and then looked all of them over again. Finally, as the four were beginning to feel very uncomfortable, she spoke.

"I'm expecting a lot of cowboys in here later. What I really need is a fresh girl for the stage show. If the lady here would do a few dances with my other girls, I'll give you a bottle of whiskey. I don't believe there is anything else I need right now."

Rizette felt surprised again that she had received the extra attention. They all looked at each other briefly, and then Oray replied.

"We would like to talk it over if that's all right."

"Yes, well, that's all right, but you shouldn't talk about it too long. The dancers start around seven o'clock, and if she decides to dance, she'll need about an hour to get ready. So, you have around three hours to decide."

After saying this, Miss Lilly walked towards the back room.

"What did she want me to do?" Rizette asked.

"She wants you to dance. That's some sort of ancient ritual. And I suspect that's where it's done." Oray pointed at the stage as he said this.

"I guess I can do that, as long as it doesn't hurt," Rizette replied.

"No. We'll try to find another way. Surely there's something we can do for some of these 'bits.' We only need two."

Oray obviously didn't like the idea of his wife doing something he wasn't familiar with. Vance and Layton studied him but kept quiet.

"We may need more than two. Is anyone else getting hungry?" Rizette held her stomach with her free hand.

"Yeah, we've not eaten for a while." Layton also put his hand to his stomach after saying this.

"Let's go look around. Surely there's something we can do to earn a few of these 'bits' we need." Vance then led the way back out the swinging doors.

The four began walking down the wooden walkway. Soon, they came to a man sitting in a chair. The man held a large paper up in front of his face.

Vance examined the paper carefully now as the man seemed unaware of their presence. When Oray and Layton noticed Vance studying the large paper, they also looked the paper over closely.

After several seconds, the man in the chair lowered the paper as if he wondered why the people hadn't walked past.

He wore one of the large hats that most of the male NLPs seemed to wear. He also had a metal star pinned on his shirt.

Vance thought this man may be able to assist them. When the man stared at the four of them, he asked.

"Excuse me, sir."

The man glanced at Vance and then over to Rizette, who still held a handful of her long dress above her knees.

"Yes, what can I do for you?"

"We're looking to earn two bits to purchase some whiskey. Do you know where we could do this? Is there anyone who needs any work done?"

The man with the metal star on his chest stared at them for several seconds. Then he spoke in a slow, deliberate voice.

"You all are not from around Dodge, are you?"

"Uhmm, well, no, sir. We're not actually from this city. We just need to earn some bits for some whiskey and maybe something to eat."

Vance's voice quivered slightly as he felt nervous that the man had so quickly become aware of them not being from this place.

Now, the man again looked at Rizette holding her dress above her knees and then continued to examine the rest of them carefully as he replied.

"It appears you all have already had more than your fair share. I'm going to warn all of you right now. I'm watching you. This is my town, and I won't allow any strange carrying on."

He then looked at the three men as if suspicious of them.

"You men aren't carrying any hidden guns, are you?"

Oray, Vance, and Layton looked at each other, and then Oray said, "No, sir. We don't have any guns."

"You better not. All guns have to be checked in with my deputy inside."

"All right, we understand." Vance began moving away after saying this. They suddenly began to understand this man was the law enforcement of the town. After getting far enough away that he couldn't hear them, Layton spoke in a whispered voice.

"That was too close. We've got to be careful. If we break the law in one of these sequences, we could be locked up and never get out of here. The others nodded in agreement.

"Did you notice the paper he held?" I saw a date of 1876." Layton continued with some bewilderment.

"I saw that, and the name 'Dodge City.' Does anyone know anything about this time and place?" Oray asked.

"This is ancient history. I don't believe any of us could know much about this sequence," Vance added as they continued to move away from the law officer.

Rizette stumbled a little in her boots but still managed to enter the conversation.

"I know this is ancient history, but I don't understand why so many of these noners know we're out of place here. They seem to know as soon as they look at us. Do we have some sort of a sign on us or something?"

Vance shook his head, also seeming stumped as he grabbed Rizette's arm to help her stay afoot. Then he replied.

"This is very serious. If we have problems in this sequence, there could be some tough consequences. Even though the military sequence was not ideal by far, it seems now to have had some advantages."

They slowly approached a man outside of what appeared to be a store. He swept the wooden walkway in front of the door with a crude broom.

Oray volunteered to speak this time.

"Sir, we need to earn a few bits. We're in need of some food and whiskey. Is there anything you need done? We would be willing to work."

The man stopped sweeping and looked the four of them over with an eye of disdain.

"I have nothing for you to do."

He then looked at Rizette standing with her dress pulled up over her knees.

"You should get her inside. She doesn't need to be walking around out here in that condition. And don't let her drink any more, for heaven's sake!" He then went back to sweeping the walkway.

The four of them moved from the store, and now Rizette appeared distraught about the entire situation.

"Let's just go back to the saloon. There's obviously something going on that we're unaware of. I'm beginning to feel very concerned about our situation."

When she said this, they stopped walking. Layton now spoke.

"She's right; we've not eaten since leaving the training sequence. Everyone around here seems to have spotted something that alerts them to our being foreigners. We don't have a clue about the location of another advisor. I think we need to go back to the saloon.

"Maybe Rizette can make a deal for some food as well as the whiskey. If we can eat and if the potion can help Oray recall more information, we might be able to get away from here, but right now, we just seem to be making our situation more dangerous."

They all knew he was right. Oray didn't like it, but he knew well they must eat, and to get into trouble in this sequence could mean disaster.

Vance said nothing but looked over to Oray.

"Yeah, all right, but if this dancing ritual is anything dangerous, she's not going to do it."

The others nodded and agreed. They all crossed the street to avoid the law officer and made their way back to the saloon.

As they walked back into the saloon, they could see several men sitting at one of the tables. The men stared down at small cards in their hands. Oray wondered about this but soon had his attention diverted as Rizette called out to Miss Lilly.

"Hello, Miss Lilly. Can I speak with you a moment?"

Miss Lilly turned from her conversation with the man who played the music.

"Yes? Oh, hello. Have you considered the offer?"

Rizette appeared to be in no mood for discussion with the others. She took control of the situation and left no room for Oray or the others to intervene.

"Yes, I've considered the offer. First, I would like to ask if we could have some food put into the deal. We've not eaten all day."

Miss Lilly thought for a second. "I believe that would be possible."

"All right. Next, I should tell you I know nothing about this 'dancing' you speak of."

After another few seconds of thought, she replied.

"Well, these are a bunch of cowhands fresh off the cattle drive. They don't know anything about dancing either, and besides, with legs like those," she pointed down to Rizette's exposed legs," all you need to do is kick them around a little, and they'll be happy."

Rizette glanced down at her exposed legs, still not understanding the connection. She didn't consider it for long, though, as her stomach demanded a quick resolution.

"I think I can handle that. I'll do it."

Miss Lilly almost appeared to smile now. "Good, I'm sure my other two girls will be happy to have some help tonight. I'll have John fetch four meals in and a bottle of whiskey. You'll need to start getting ready soon, so don't drink too much."

After sitting down at a table, Oray expressed frustration. "You should have let us talk about it first, Riz."

"No, I shouldn't have, Ray. We're all tired and hungry. You're not the only one who can take chances for the team. Besides, I'm the one doing the 'dancing' or kicking, or whatever it is. I'm hungry, and I need to eat. I'm sure I can just follow along with the other girls. It can't be that hard."

Oray grimaced a little but had nothing else to say. He was also very hungry, and he knew Vance and Layton had to be as well.

A bit later, John brought four plates of food and a large bottle of whiskey. The food was nothing like they had ever eaten, but it tasted very good nonetheless. After eating all the food, they sat staring at the large bottle of amber-colored liquid. Oray picked one of the tiny glasses up that John had brought.

"I suppose we take small drinks of this stuff?"

"We, what do you mean by that? You take small drinks of it," Vance replied quickly.

Oray now gave him a look of surprise.

"You're going to drink some too, right?"

"I don't know about that. You're the one who can't remember the access information, not me and not Layton or Rizette."

Oray seemed a bit betrayed.

"Well, if this stuff tastes delicious, I'm not telling you guys. I'll just drink it all myself."

As they spoke about this, several rough-looking men came in and went straight to the long table. They spoke with John, and he brought them something to drink.

Vance turned back to Oray after they had watched the men for a few seconds.

"We'll watch you first." He then pulled the plug from the bottle and smelled it. His face automatically twisted from the smell. He then tried to recover quickly as he realized Oray watched him closely.

"Is it that bad?" Oray asked.

"No, it's uh, not too bad," Vance replied as he poured the little glass full and handed it to Oray.

The three watched him closely as he took the small glass. He smelled it and immediately pulled it away from his nose as if the smell had tried to bite him.

"Not that bad, then what would you call it?" After Oray said this, Rizette took the bottle from the table and smelled it. Her face immediately reacted with discomfort from the smell.

"Aagh, you think this stuff will actually work?" She looked at Vance and Layton, indicating an answer from either one would suffice. Vance replied.

"I don't know. But we don't seem to have many options at this point. We need more information about the creed and hopefully the second access word. I suppose if this doesn't work, we can look for an advisor tomorrow. Either way, I don't think we should hang around this sequence any longer than we must. Apparently, we are quite out of place here, and everyone seems to be aware of it."

Rizette reacted as if accepting this answer and put the bottle back on the table. However, Oray continued to examine the small glass of whiskey with apprehension.

"That's easy for you to say, Vance. You don't have to drink this stuff."

Now, Layton joined the conversation.

"Come on Oray. It's just a little bitty drink. These people drink this stuff all the time. Surely it's not so bad."

Oray's face remained strained from the smell of the whiskey he held in his hand. He then glanced down at it and, with one quick movement, drank the small dose all at once. He coughed and moved back in his chair, putting the small glass on the table as he tried to catch his breath.

"Aghhh, that's awful. I can't believe these people drink this stuff!!"

"Shhh," Vance tried to get Oray to settle down a little as the commotion had caused the others in the saloon to look their way.

Oray now glanced around and, noticing the people in the saloon were looking at him, lowered his voice and pulled his chair back up to the table.

"That's terrible. It tastes worse than it smells if that's possible."

Right after he said this, Miss Lilly and one of the girls in a colorful dress walked up to the table.

"All right, uhmm," she looked at Rizette with her hand out as if waiting for a name.

"Rizette."

"All right, Rizette, this is Prissy. You'll need to get ready now. She has some extra outfits and will loan you one. Just follow along with the other girls, and you'll be fine."

"I'll do that. And thank you, Miss Lilly."

She then actually smiled for the first time and replied, "You're welcome," after which she walked back towards the long table.

"I guess I need to go," Rizette stood up and waved a little goodbye to Oray as she left with Prissy.

A few minutes after Rizette left, Oray stared at the bottle on the table.

"You know, I think I know why these people drink this stuff."

"Why?" Layton asked.

"It sort of makes you feel good after a while."

"Really?" Layton asked again with interest.

"Yeah, I think I'll have another drink." He picked up the bottle and poured another drink.

As he did this, more men came into the saloon. These men appeared to be in a very good mood and were yelling out to John for whiskey.

Oray downed the small drink and again coughed a little. This time, however, he didn't push away from the table. After he set the bottle down, Vance picked it up and smelled it again.

"So, do you think it'll help your memory?" Vance asked as he sat the bottle back down.

"It might. I know I'm feeling something. I think it'll help. But it sure does taste bad." Oray's eyes appeared a little glazed when he said this. Again, more men came into the saloon, which was about half full now.

In the back of the saloon, Prissy pulled several of her colorful dresses out for Rizette to pick from.

"You must be from out East. You and your friends don't act like you're from around these parts." She held a dress up and looked it over as she said this to Rizette.

"Yes, we're from the, ah, East. You're very perceptive."

"I want ta go out East sometime, maybe to New York or Charleston. Is that where you all are from?"

"Yeah, we're from there," Rizette replied as she began trying on one of the dresses.

"Which one?" Prissy turned and asked with a puzzled expression.

"The uhm, second one," Rizette couldn't remember the places Prissy said and tried to act as if she were busy with the dress.

"Charleston?"

"Yes, Charleston," she replied as she adjusted the dress and tried to think of some way to get off the conversation.

"I would just love to see Charleston. I'll bet it's beautiful." Prissy seemed to glow at the mere thought of Charleston.

"Oh, yes, it is lovely. I do like this, uhm, outfit much better than that other one. At least this one isn't hanging over your legs so much." Rizette examined the colorful dress that only hung down to her knees. "This is much more comfortable."

Prissy giggled a little. "Yeah, and the cowboys sure like them better too."

Rizette didn't understand this comment but thought it better just to smile and nod as if she did.

"Now, we need to fix your hair and face."

Prissy had Rizette sit down, and she began to work on her hair. Then, after putting her hair up and placing colorful ribbons in it, she began putting powder on her face. Rizette thought this to be unusual but sat still until Prissy finished.

While this occurred in a backstage room, Oray had finished two more drinks of whiskey in the hopes of improving his memory.

Having completed her preparations for the upcoming dances, Rizette came out front to check on Oray.

Vance and Layton stared at Oray with obvious dismay as she walked up to the table.

"Wow, look at you." Vance noticed her first.

"Yeah, you look great, Rizette," Layton added.

"Well, this one is at least more comfortable. It doesn't hang all the way to the ground. I hate the way that other one hangs on my legs." She twirled the dress a little as she said this.

Then, she sat down and looked at Oray. He sat in the chair with a blank and glazed expression on his face. She studied him closer as he didn't appear very alert at all.

"So, is there any progress with his memory?"

Vance and Layton looked at each other a little nervously when she asked this. Then Vance replied.

"Maybe, you should uhm, ask him, Riz."

She glanced at Vance and appeared a bit puzzled when he said this. Then she turned back to Oray.

"Can you remember anything else about the access information, Ray?"

Oray looked up and then at her. His head bobbled some as he stared at her. Then he blurted out.

"Who are you?"

Rizette's face contorted when he said this. She turned to Vance and Layton, who both expressed embarrassment. She then turned back to Oray.

"I'm your wife!"

He smiled slyly as his head continued to bobble. He looked over at Vance and laughed or grunted. With slurred speech, he said.

"Awesome, I've gots me a hottie wife!" He then leaned forward a little, and his head continued to slowly descend until his forehead settled on the table with a light thud.

Rizette quickly lifted his head and opened an eye. He laughed a little. She let his head go back to the table.

"I don't think that stuff is helping his memory at all."

"No, I don't think so either," Vance said in a rather embarrassed and meek tone.

"Nope, it seems to be a dead-end," Layton added quickly.

"Rizette!" Prissy called out across the now, very crowded saloon. When Rizette looked at her, Prissy motioned for her to come backstage.

"I've got to go. You guys stay with him. Don't let him drink any more of that stuff." She stood up and moved towards the backstage area.

Rizette was already growing upset about Oray as she made her way towards the stage area. So, when a cowboy grabbed the back of her dress and pulled her towards him, she reacted as if she were still in the combat sequence and used the momentum to her advantage.

Rizette doubled her fist as he pulled her. She turned and struck him square in the face. The cowboy never realized what had hit him. He thought he was grabbing a dance hall girl but got hold of a woman that had just spent several months in a combat zone. The cowboy landed on the floor and didn't get up for a while. Rizette shook her hand to alleviate the pain from hitting his face. She then turned back towards the stage.

The entire saloon erupted in laughter from this, and though she didn't realize it at that moment, this punch set the tone for the rest of the evening.

When she arrived backstage, Prissy and the other girl both appeared somewhat nervous. Prissy held onto the other girl as she peered out to the saloon from the corner of the stage.

"You sure woke them up, Rizette," Prissy said as she watched Rizette investigate her sore hand.

"Hmm, oh yeah. Well, he shouldn't have grabbed me like that."

Prissy smiled a little and seemed to admire Rizette for her ability to knock a cowboy out. But she remained nervous.

"Well, I've got a feeling it's going to be a rough night."

Rizette's attention now moved to Prissy and the other dance hall girl.

"Why do you say that?"

"Oh, I don't know." Prissy then glanced out to the rowdy saloon again and continued. "I guess you could call it 'woman's intuition.'"

Rizette appeared puzzled by this.

"What's 'woman's intuition'?"

Prissy glanced at her and smiled a little about her lack of knowledge.

"That's a special feeling a woman can have about something. Women often have feelings about things that men don't. It's our little advantage, I guess you could say."

Rizette appeared to give this some thought.

Then, Prissy took hold of her arm and said with a nervous voice, "Are we ready for this?"

Rizette didn't understand why the two women seemed so nervous. They looked as if the three of them were about to charge an enemy gun emplacement.

"Yeah, sure, I'm ready," she replied calmly.

"All right then, let's go do this." The other girl took Rizette's opposite arm so that the three had locked arms, with Rizette in the middle. They moved out onto the lit stage, and Rizette suddenly received a massive dose of the very unfamiliar feeling of stage fright.

Though she had just come from the saloon floor, everything appeared completely different up on the stage.

The cowboys yelled and whistled. The piano began playing a loud banging rhythm, and as she was trying to grasp this dramatic change, the girls on both sides of her began kicking their legs out and twirling their skirts up and down to the music.

Rizette stumbled around at first and then tried to kick her legs about as well, but she could barely function in this completely foreign environment.

If Oray had been in any condition to watch, he'd have had little doubt that his wife would have much rather been in the combat zone fighting the black-uniformed soldiers than in this situation.

Yet, she soldiered on as the cowboys yelled loudly and rolled bottles onto the stage; a few tried to grab the girls' legs. The three would simply dance back a way to stay out of reach. After about fifteen minutes of dancing, they finally stopped. To Rizette it felt like an hour.

Out of breath and sweating, she staggered a little to the backstage area. Once she was able to breathe a bit more normally, she went to check on Oray. Several of the cowboys grabbed at her behind and received a swift punch in the face from her. This just stirred up laughter and seemed to encourage them even more.

She sat down at the table where Oray still lay with his head on the table. As she continued to catch her breath, she said to Vance and Layton.

"I was so wrong. This is going to be very, very difficult."

The two men simply stared at the strange sight of this completely different woman they'd never seen before.

As a cowboy came by and tried to reach down and fondle her, she quickly backhanded him, and he moved along.

Realizing that Vance and Layton now watched her with slightly shocked expressions on their faces, she shook her head a little in a puzzled manner and asked, "What?"

The remainder of the night consisted of Rizette fighting off cowboys and dancing until her legs ached. She would periodically check on Oray, who seemed to fade in and out. When he was conscious, he appeared not to know who or where he was.

The madness finally ended for Rizette around midnight when the saloon closed. She changed back into her dress, and they carried Oray out of the saloon.

All four sat exhausted on the hard, wooden walkway. They leaned against the wall of a building and tried to sleep.

As the sun crept up the following morning, Oray began to moan.

"Ohhhh, I'm sick."

Rizette moved and felt her entire body ache, particularly her legs. Yet, she took Oray in her arms and held him as a mother would a child.

"Ohh... my head... and my stomach... What in the world did that stuff do to me?"

Vance held the remnants of the corked whiskey bottle up as if trying to see something inside that they may have missed before.

"Well, it certainly didn't help your memory," he said.

"I told you those old-world potions had side effects." Rizette now sounded very concerned for her husband as she tried to comfort him.

As all four began to move about, a woman in a dress like the one Rizette wore walked up. She made an extra effort to move around them.

"Excuse me, miss. My husband is very sick. Where can I take him to get some help?"

When Rizette asked her this, she looked down at the four of them. She seemed particularly interested in the whiskey bottle Vance held in his hand.

"All of you should go down to the church at the end of this street. That's the only place people like you will get any help." She then walked away briskly.

"What did she mean 'people like us'?" Layton asked, but all four were wondering about it.

"I don't know, but maybe we should try the place. I think that whiskey may have poisoned me."

Oray obviously felt very bad.

They struggled to their feet with the three trying to help Oray up. A night on the wooden walkway made them hurt all over. As they walked in the direction the woman pointed, the town began to wake up. Horses and wagons passed by noisily.

After what became a long, painful struggle, the small group reached a building with a sign in front indicating it was a church. They staggered up the steps and through the door.

Inside, they only saw rows of pews and the pulpit in front of these pews. They maneuvered to one of the rear pews and helped Oray lay down.

"I don't see anyone here. Do you think the woman told us the right place?"

Rizette now began to feel the pains of an empty stomach. She knew they were all in bad shape due to their experiences since arriving in this sequence.

Layton sat down and obviously felt bad as well. He'd been less and less active as the days went by. Rizette wondered how long they could survive in this environment.

Just as she began to feel depression settling inside her, a man walked into the church from a door at the front; noticing the four at the back of the church, he moved towards them

"Can I help you?"

"My husband is sick! We've only had one small meal in two days. Can you help us please?"

Rizette had never begged before, and this had the strong sensation of begging. But she didn't care. They all needed help.

The well-dressed man walked cautiously back towards them. When the man stood close, he examined them with interest. After a moment of looking the four over, he finally spoke.

"I'm Pastor Harrison. I'll provide the four of you with something to eat if you'll just give me that bottle of whiskey."

Vance glanced down at the bottle in his hand. He then held it up to the pastor without hesitation.

"There, now you see. That wasn't so difficult, was it?"

Pastor Harrison took the bottle from Vance's hand.

"If you'll follow me, I'll get some coffee and breakfast for you."

Rizette helped Oray up, and Vance helped Layton. They followed Pastor Harrison through the church. They went out a door that was past the pulpit. Outside, and across a path, stood a house that was behind the church.

As they entered the house, they saw a woman washing dishes.

"This is my wife, Velma." The woman said hello with a soft voice. "Velma, these people need something to eat. Can we get them some coffee and some breakfast?"

Velma dried her hands on her apron and helped Rizette get Oray to sit down at the table.

"Thank you," Rizette said as her husband sat down.

"I'll get some coffee for all of you and then prepare some breakfast." Velma poured them some black coffee and went to work cooking the four some breakfast.

Although Rizette was unfamiliar with coffee prepared in this rather crude fashion, it tasted great and seemed to give her an energy burst she desperately needed. Oray sipped his coffee and appeared to gain some strength from it.

Pastor Harrison drifted in and out of the small dining area as the four ate their meal. It looked as if he were trying to stay busy until they finished eating. Once they were done eating, they all drank more coffee and talked.

"Are you feeling better?" Rizette put her hand on Oray's shoulder as he sipped his coffee.

"Yeah, the breakfast and this coffee helped a lot. I still don't feel completely normal, but much better."

Vance spoke up now.

"One thing's for certain, we've got to get out of this sequence as soon as possible. With all the rituals and traditions during this period, there's no telling what we're doing wrong. Obviously, we're doing something unusual, and the NLPs here can identify us as abnormal."

After saying this, he took a drink of his coffee, and the others considered what he had said.

Then Rizette commented. "Last night, Prissy noticed I wasn't from here within a matter of minutes." The four again sipped their coffee and considered the situation.

Pastor Harrison ventured back in and, seeing they had finished breakfast, pulled a chair up to the table and sat down with them.

"Was the meal all right?"

"Yes, it was wonderful. Thank you so much." Rizette replied with gratitude, and the others agreed.

"You're very welcome." Then Pastor Harrison appeared to be briefly in thought before going on.

"I would really like to help all of you more. That's if you're willing to try to help yourself as well. You all seem to have so much potential. I hate to see young people get caught up in the vices of this world and waste the potential they have inside them."

The four sat listening to Pastor Harrison but not being exactly sure what he was getting at. After he finished saying this, he sat quietly and appeared to be waiting for their response.

Finally, Vance struggled to make a comment simply to appease Pastor Harrison.

"We appreciate your concern, sir. We do need help, but I believe you've done all you can for us. The meal was a tremendous contribution."

Then, casually and almost under his breath, Vance said. "What we really need right now is an advisor."

Pastor Harrison perked up a little when Vance said this.

"Well, I may not be the best in the world, but I feel I am an acceptable advisor. My congregation at least seems to feel so."

When he said this, all four immediately sat up and glanced at each other in disbelief. Then, they turned and stared at Pastor Harrison.

Velma came in and broke the strained silence as she poured the pastor some coffee. He took a drink, sat the cup back down, and looked back curiously at his four guests.

Oray glanced at the other three quickly as if wanting confirmation. He then turned to Pastor Harrison and spoke in a plain, monotone voice.

"Oray 536, I wish to access Monitor."

Pastor Harrison's face went blank. He stood up in a mechanical manner and walked straight to the door.

The four stood up and followed him out the door and back into the church. He went into a small office, and there stood a tall wardrobe cabinet.

Still having a blank expression, he opened the door, and immediately the light of the virtual doorway shone into the office and lit everything inside.

Still appearing in disbelief, Oray looked around at the lit-up faces of the others. "Are we ready?"

"I'm ready. Let's get out of this place." Rizette took his arm as she said this. The others locked arms as they had done before and went into the doorway. Again, they found themselves in the well-lit turnstile.

CHAPTER EIGHT:

VIVA LA FRANCE

Gazing around at the doors, they knew that once again they must choose a doorway, with no idea where they might land. After everyone had silently studied the doors, Oray spoke.

"So, does anyone have a suggestion?"

Vance slowly walked from door to door, and Rizette and Oray fell in behind. Layton agreed to stay by the door they had just walked through. They examined the doors one by one but found nothing to indicate any difference.

After making the full circle and arriving back to Layton, Vance said. "We're completely dependent on luck, it seems. There's nothing to help us decide.

"So, what if we let Rizette pick this time? Maybe a woman will have better luck." Layton smiled a little at her when he said this. She gave him a strange expression and replied.

"Maybe, but I may also pick a worse sequence. Why don't one of you guys pick?" They stood looking at each other for a minute.

Then, Oray seemed to run out of patience. Walking over to a random door, he opened it.

"Let's take this one and go. It can't be any worse than where we just came from."

They all glanced at each other, and since no one made an objection, they locked arms and went through.

A cold, hard rain fell on all four as the virtual door closed behind them. They tried to focus their eyes to see in the stormy darkness. The familiar sounds of war rang out not far from them.

Then, as they became aware of a stream of people passing by them, an artillery shell came hurtling in close. All the people fell to protect themselves. Realizing what was happening, the four fell to the ground also, just before the shell exploded close by. Once the danger was past, all four became even more aware of their dire situation.

Mud oozed all around them as they tried to pull themselves from the quagmire of an over-traveled dirt road, drenched by an abundance of rain. As they pulled themselves up from the cold, muddy ground, Rizette looked at her husband with a bit of frustration. She raked some mud from her face before almost yelling out to him.

"What was that you were saying about couldn't be any worse?"

Oray shrugged his shoulders with an expression of apology.

They stared into the wet darkness, struggling to see anything to help their situation.

"Where are we?" Rizette asked as the rain fell hard onto her face. Then, another shell came screaming by. They squatted down this time, seeming reluctant to go back into the cold mud.

From the stream of people passing by, Vance noticed most were either walking or in a small cart pulled by a horse. Then, as all four stood back up and expressed shock at their predicament, they heard a beeping sound.

Along the muddy road came some type of vehicle. Slowly, the odd motorized monstrosity crept up to them and then slipped and slid past as they watched, in rain-soaked curiosity.

"That looks like the, what did Riley call it, a 'tin Lizzy'?" Rizette asked and again wiped mud and rain from her face.

"Yeah, I think so," Oray replied. "So, this must be early twentieth century."

Oray also tried to clear mud from his face after saying this, then continued.

"We've got to find some shelter. Come on, let's go this way. It seems all the people are trying to get away from the battle. That's probably a good idea."

As soon as he said this, gunfire from an automatic weapon came not far away and in the opposite direction that everyone moved in.

They began slogging along in the mud and rain. The people they walked with appeared depressed and hopeless as they carried their meager possessions or small children in their arms.

An odd honking sound now came from in front of them. Slowly, the sounds of another motorized vehicle came closer.

"Viva La France!" Someone could be heard yelling. Then as the vehicle passed by in the direction of the battle, they could see it was loaded down with soldiers.

Vance looked at Oray, who watched the odd sight with equal puzzlement. They continued, and soon more soldiers were seen walking in the rain and mud, all headed towards the battle.

The night crept by slowly and cold. The rain eventually stopped, but the cold continued. Rizette shivered, and Layton began to fall behind. Oray helped Rizette and Vance began helping Layton.

After they had walked the remainder of the evening and then all night to create some space between themselves and the battle, they came to a small village as morning began to break over the horizon.

Searching around the half-empty village, Oray found a small barn; he then went back to where the other three were and escorted them to it.

Cold, wet, tired, and hungry, they huddled together as once again the sounds of war rang out in the distance. Layton appeared to be in a depleted condition as he lay in the dirty hay on the ground.

"Hang in there, buddy." Vance patted Layton on the chest. Layton coughed, and his breath streamed out in a mist due to the colder temperature. He began to speak, and the others gathered around him in a show of camaraderie.

"I know what's happening to me. I saw it happen to Carl. He was the third diver Oray's assistant spoke of. He faded out before you showed up, Vance."

He then coughed again several times before continuing.

"I never said anything to you, Vance. I didn't want you to give up like he did. He'd become very depressed when I found him in the military training sequence. He'd already been there a while. I tried to cheer him up, but he'd already begun to lose hope. Then he began to fade, just as I'm doing now. But I haven't given up hope. I want to make it a little longer. I want to... I want to know who did this to us."

Rizette turned away as several tears ran down her face. She held her mouth to muffle the sounds of weeping. It didn't work completely, as the others knew she was crying. Oray put his hand on Layton's shoulder, and Vance squeezed his arm.

"We're going to find out. You hang in there because we're going to find out who did this." As soon as Vance said this, Oray stood up.

"I'm going to find an advisor. We've got to get him out of here." He then walked out of the barn. Rizette jumped up and followed him.

Coming up beside him, she took his arm. "We've got to make it out. We've got to make it for Layton's sake." She wiped tears from her eyes as they walked briskly through the village.

Oray didn't reply to his wife, but at that instant, the determination doubled inside him. Layton and Carl deserved better than this.

A few villagers were packing their belongings in preparation to leave. Oray and Rizette approached an older man and his wife as they loaded a small hand-drawn cart.

"Excuse me. We're looking for an advisor." As soon as Oray said this, the man began waving his hand as if to wave them away.

"No, no, I don't have time right now. Don't you know the Germans are coming? You should leave right away." He then went swiftly back into the house as his wife came out with several valuables to place in the cart.

Oray and Rizette continued through the village. As they did so, the sounds of war increased in the distance. The battle sounds were growing closer. Oray stopped and knocked on a door. No one answered, so they moved on.

A shell burst directly outside of town. People hurriedly passed by as they attempted to leave.

"Excuse me. Excuse me. We need to find an advisor. Could you help us?"

Oray sounded more desperate now. As more people began to pass by, Rizette joined in and began asking them also. The people paid little attention to them. If they did listen to the question, they acted as if Oray and Rizette were crazy rather than give an answer. Many would simply tell them they should leave right away.

Another shell screamed in, landing in town this time, the ground shook under their feet. Rizette stopped an elderly lady with an old bag in her hand.

"Please help us. We need to find the advisor."

The woman seemed bewildered by Rizette's question, but she replied quickly.

"That would be the counselor on the edge of town." She pointed her age-weathered finger in the direction. "He lives in the large gray and red house on the right. But I doubt he's still there." She then pulled herself from Rizette's grasp and moved away quickly.

Another shell landed on the edge of town, causing screams from some women and children around them.

"Ray, I know where the advisor is!" she yelled out to Oray, who still attempted to get an answer from the passing people. He nodded, and Rizette darted towards the house on the edge of town. Oray followed behind.

As they approached the house, they saw a man in a suit loading a small wagon. A woman also dressed nicely raced back and forth, busily loading items from the house into the wagon. They spoke in small bursts as they passed each other.

"Did you get the black case? It has the important papers."

In and out of the house, they darted.

"Excuse me; we need to speak with you." Oray tried to catch a breath at the same time as he spoke to the counselor.

"No. No. Get away! I have no time to speak with anyone now! The Germans are right outside of town! Are you crazy? You should be leaving now." The counselor put a bag in the small wagon and began to turn and go back into the house.

"Oray 536, I wish to access Monitor."

The counselor stopped, and his face went blank. His wife stood frozen as well, staring blankly into space. Then, the counselor walked mechanically into the house. Oray and Rizette followed him through the disheveled dwelling to an office in the back. There stood a large cabinet. He opened it, and the virtual door revealed itself.

"All right, you stay with him. I'll go get Vance and Layton." Immediately after Oray said this, another shell landed very close. The entire house shook, and the glass windows rattled in their framework. Rizette coughed and tried to shoo away the dust and small debris that fell from the ceiling.

"All right, but hurry, and be careful!"

Oray nodded and darted towards the front door. As he came to the door, an army ambulance drove by quickly, and other military vehicles followed behind on their way to the nearby battle. Shells were now landing all around the town, and gunshots were going off close by.

Then, the counselor's wife began to move again just as Oray started down the steps.

"Oray! Oray!" Rizette called from the back room. He turned and darted back through the house. The counselor was yelling at her, and the cabinet door was closed.

"You people are insane! We've got to get out of here! What do you want anyway?"

"Oray 536, I wish to access Monitor."

The counselor again stopped, and his face went blank. He again opened the cabinet door, and the light of the virtual doorway streamed into the small room.

"You're going to have to stay here, Ray. The door closed as soon as you got to the front of the house. I'll go get Vance and Layton." Rizette almost yelled to be heard over the increasing battle noises. She turned to move towards the front door as more dust and debris fell from the ceiling. The shells were falling closer and more frequently.

"Riz!"

She stopped and turned back.

Oray wanted to say something but didn't know what to say. He looked into his wife's eyes. She gazed into his. She then ran into his arms, and they kissed as if it might be the last kiss. Then she quickly pulled away from him and ran through the house and into the chaotic streets.

Shells landed close by, one after another. Army vehicles and horse-drawn wagons crowded the streets, all struggling as they proceeded to or away from the battle closing in on the town.

Rizette labored through the streets, dodging people and soldiers. Then a shell landed close by, and the impact threw her to the ground. Debris fell on top of her already dirty clothes. She stood back up and stumbled as exhaustion began to take hold. Again, she moved through the chaos. People pushed her as panic began to grip everyone fleeing the battle.

An army car almost ran over her; she had to fall away from the metal vehicle, so it wouldn't hit her. Rizette gasped for breath. The air chilled her weary lungs. She became disoriented and scanned the area in a desperate search for the small barn.

Again, she stood up and ran, forcing her legs to move one step after another.

Finally, she arrived at the small barn and became shocked by the sight she beheld.

Wounded soldiers lay all around the outside of the weathered structure. Gunfire was very close by, and many soldiers moved around the area. Rizette called out as soon as she came close.

"Vance, Layton!" She tried to catch her breath.

Vance came out with Layton holding onto his shoulder.

"Come on. We found the advisor, but we've got to hurry. Oray is trying to keep him there."

The three moved along the streets that were now a mass of chaos and confusion. Shells began landing relentlessly and directly into the town.

They fell to the ground just as one demolished a house in front of them. Then they got up, but the mass of debris caused them more delay.

What would have simply been a few minutes of travel turned into ten minutes of hell.

Oray paced back and forth in the crumbling house. He could barely contain himself as the battle outside became more intense by the minute. The desire to run out and search for Rizette was only tempered by a certainty the counselor would leave as soon as he was out of the house. He felt as if his insides were about to blow apart. Another shell landed close by. More dust and debris fell from the ceiling. Where could they be?

Then Rizette called out to him from the front door. His heart felt as if it received a burst of air by the sound of her voice. He shouted back as they struggled into the wreckage of the house.

No sooner did they make it through the front of the house than a shell removed it entirely, causing all but the spellbound counselor to fall to the floor from the impact.

"Quick, let's go." Oray took Rizette's arm as she took Layton's, and Vance quickly took Layton's other arm and moved through the virtual doorway. Once inside, the doorway closed, and a sudden silence fell around them.

Rizette looked down to see her muddied clothes had again changed into the light gray overalls. They were still hungry and exhausted, but relief came over them as they sat down on the floor to collect themselves.

After catching their breath and regaining some strength, Vance slowly stood up.

"Like it or not, we've got to go through another door soon. We haven't eaten anything for who knows how long, and Layton needs help."

Layton lay on the floor in an exhausted state. Oray and Rizette gazed out at the assortment of doors.

Then Oray said in a tired voice, "Riz, I think you're up."

"What, why do I have to pick?" She expressed obvious reluctance.

"Vance suggested the first door. I picked the second. Layton is in no shape to pick. It's your turn, my love."

Oray gave her a look she'd become familiar with.

She breathed out in an expression of gambling her last bit of money.

"All right, but if it's a lousy pick, just remember you guys are the ones who wanted me to pick."

Vance spoke now as he leaned down on his knees, still trying to catch his breath.

"That sounds fair enough. But I wouldn't worry too much Riz, considering the actual situation, we seem to be at the mercy of luck no matter who picks. We're all aware of that."

Now she appeared to calm down some.

She stood up and went slowly around the doors. After passing one up, she came back to it. Then she continued and walked past the others. When she'd walked past all the doors other than the one they just came through, she went back to the door she had checked twice.

"This one," she pointed at the door.

"Why that one?" Oray asked.

"Just call it a woman's intuition."

Vance and Oray looked at each other with puzzled expressions. Vance shrugged his shoulders.

"Sounds good to me." Then he went to help Layton up.

Oray came over and helped with Layton. They moved to the door. Oray opened it, and they locked arms in the fashion that had now become almost automatic. Through the door and into the light they went.

Sunshine was a welcome first sight for the four weary travelers, particularly after the previous sequence.

As things cleared more, they could see green trees and heard the songs of birds. A few seconds later, the scene presented a pleasant view of freshly cut green grass, green leafy trees, and what appeared to be swings and other devices for children to play on.

Then an automobile drove past on a road not far from them. It was much more advanced than the "tin Lizzy" they had seen in the previous sequence.

As all four tried to take in the obviously more hospitable environment, Oray made the first comment.

"We should have tried that 'woman's intuition thing' a lot sooner."

Vance gazed at the scene and added, "You got that right."

Rizette smiled a little, but inside she felt a great relief that this sequence wasn't worse than the last one.

As they began to move across the grass, Rizette looked down and was again pleased to find she wore pants rather than the heavy, cumbersome dresses of the two previous sequences. The pants were rather tight but still easier to move around in.

Assisting Layton, they walked with some effort until coming to a bench. On the bench sat a man dressed in worn and weathered clothing. He had a short beard and appeared to be around fifty to sixty years old.

"Excuse me, sir. We're in need of some shelter and food. Do you know where we can find any? This man needs to eat and rest."

The elderly man looked at Vance when he said this. He then looked at the others, seeming a little puzzled.

"You need to find a shelter?"

"Yes, sir," Vance replied.

"Well, I go down to the fourth street shelter. They have pretty good food, and the beds are clean."

"Could you direct us to this place?"

"Yeah, it's about five blocks down this street. It's the brick building on the corner. You'll see a sign."

"Thank you, sir. Thank you."

The others also repeated thanks to the man after Vance, and they moved in the direction he'd given.

While moving along the sidewalk, and as automobiles passed by, they gazed around at the more familiar scenes and buildings.

"This must be early twenty-first century," Vance said.

"I think it may be late twentieth century," Oray added as he tried to spot familiar items from time spent in the antique shop.

Vance continued.

"Either way, this is a much more hospitable environment than the last two sequences."

Oray grunted an "uh-huh" in agreement with the statement as they crossed a street. Soon, they arrived at the shelter the man told them about.

"This is going to cost money. And we don't have any."

"We've got to get Layton some help," Rizette replied to Oray.

"We'll work or whatever to pay for the help, even if I have to dance again. We've got to get him something to eat and a place to rest."

They went into the building, almost carrying Layton, who now appeared to be in an almost desperate condition.

As they walked into the building, a man noticed them. He stopped talking with another older man and moved towards them.

"Can I help you?"

"Our friend needs some help. He hasn't eaten in almost two days. He needs to rest also. We don't have any money, but the rest of us will work for you if there is something we can do."

Vance sounded more desperate than Oray or Rizette had ever heard him sound. They realized Layton was likely the closest friend he had. The harsh environment of the military training sequence must have forged a bond between them.

"Yes, well, don't worry about money. Is he sick, or do you know what's wrong with him?" The man tried to get a better look at Layton as he slumped over Vance's shoulder.

"I believe he's just exhausted and hungry. He needs to rest in a bed and eat something."

"Bring him back this way. We'll get him into a bed."

The man moved towards the back of the building and, after passing through a double doorway, came to an open bay area with rows of beds.

"Sit him here."

Vance and Oray sat Layton on a bed and gently laid him back.

"I'll get him something to eat." The man went to a door at the back of the building and soon returned with a bowl of soup and a small package of crackers. Vance sat down and began to feed Layton as a nurse might feed a patient.

Oray and Rizette sat on a bed beside them and watched with concern.

"My name is Mark Stevens, by the way. I'm the full-time host here at the shelter."

"I'm Oray, and this is my wife, Rizette."

Vance then turned from feeding Layton and said quickly, "Vance."

"Well, it's nice to meet all of you."

Mark studied the three for a few minutes, then after examining Oray, Rizette, and Vance for a short while, he reacted as if suddenly realizing something.

"How long has it been since you three have eaten?"

They glanced at each other, and Oray replied weakly, "Uhm, almost two days, I think."

"Good Lord, you should have told me! I'll get you something right away." Mark jumped up and hurried to the back again.

Soon, he returned with a tray and three bowls of soup along with several packages of crackers. After sitting this down, he went back and retrieved some beverages.

"You all look as if you've been through the wringer."

Oray glanced up from his soup. He looked over at Vance with a puzzled expression. Vance was also eating but tried to make a neutral response, realizing neither Oray nor he had any idea what this "wringer" was.

"You could say that, I suppose. I would say we've had an eventful episode of activities." He then went back to eating his soup.

Mark had an odd expression after Vance's statement.

"Yes, well, that is a very colorful way to put it. At any rate, I'm glad you found your way here. I hope your friend recovers soon."

Oray finished the last of his soup and, after taking a quick drink of his canned soda, decided to try to keep the conversation on their terms.

"May we stay here tonight with our friend?"

"Yes, you can do that; I insist. In fact, you can stay in these beds close by your friend if you wish, but no 'hanky panky,' all right?"

After Mark said this, Oray struggled to decipher the 'hanky panky' term. He then tried to think of something to stay in line with the conversation.

"We'll work to pay our way here. Vance and I can do cleaning or whatever you need done."

Mark chuckled about this.

"Well, I might take you up on some help as far as the cleaning goes. That is very considerate of you. You can pay me, though, by getting back on your own feet. I'll feel compensated when you get back to work and find a place of your own. This shelter is for helping people get back to self-sufficiency. That's our reward, to see people become productive citizens again. Unfortunately, too many of our guests want to make this their full-time residence. I hope you all can become self-sufficient again soon. That'll be payment enough for me."

As Rizette put her bowl back on the tray, Oray looked at Vance, and then they both glanced at Rizette as if making some form of decision without words. Then Vance replied.

"We'll do that for you, Mark Stevens. We may need a little assistance getting started, but we'll stay with it and learn fast. Don't worry; you'll be compensated for your generosity."

Oray and Rizette nodded in agreement with Vance's statement.

Mark still appeared somewhat puzzled by this. He again chuckled a little as if trying to make sure they weren't making fun of him. When no one else laughed, he decided they were just a little out of the ordinary.

"Yes, well, that's good to hear. I'll be looking forward to that. And I can direct you to the labor office as well as help you find housing once you get working again."

The three stared at him now as if waiting for more conversation, so he tried to add something else. "And I'll do whatever else I can to help you get back on your feet."

When he said this, Rizette glanced down at her feet, which were firmly on the floor. She then looked back up to Mark and said, "We're very grateful for your assistance, Mark Stevens."

"All right then, the showers are in the back, and there are separate showers for men and women, again, no hanky panky, please. You'll see the towels on racks outside the showers. Breakfast is at 7:00am, and if you're not here when it's served, you'll have to wait until lunch to eat. My room is in the far back, but I ask that you please not disturb me for trivial things. Is there anything else I can do for you right now?"

They glanced at each other quickly, and then Oray spoke. "You've been a great help already. We won't bother you with anything else at this time."

"Okay. Well, I hope you all get some rest. I'm sure I'll see you tomorrow." Mark then stood up and went to the back room.

Layton had fallen asleep after eating. The three of them sat quietly and considered their situation for a few seconds. Then Vance spoke first.

"We've got to try to blend in here and get Layton well. This appears to be the best situation we've come into yet."

Oray nodded. "I agree. We seem to be holding our own with Mark Stevens. If we can get an operation base, maybe we can utilize some of the technology here to help us."

Vance made a sour face. "I doubt they have much technology worth using in this period. But I agree, this is certainly our best option so far and there may be something we can find to help. I think we have a better chance of survival here than the last two sequences."

As Oray and Vance talked, Rizette examined the large bay and the beds. Several people in scruffy clothes had entered and were settling into beds of their choice.

Then she spoke while still gazing about the building.

"We'll need to work somehow. We've only got the clothes we arrived in. Also, I don't think Layton should work. He needs to take it easy."

They glanced back at their sleeping friend.

"Vance and I can work. Maybe you can stay with Layton. We can start looking around tomorrow. If we can stay here a few days, maybe we can get adjusted to the environment and then secure some work for money."

They all agreed with Oray's statement. Then he pushed one of the single beds together with another one, and he and Rizette lay down on top of the blankets in each other's arms as their days in the military training sequence were still fresh in their memory.

Vance also lay down in a bed on the other side of Layton, and they all slept well for the first time in days.

The following day, Vance and Oray ventured out as Rizette stayed at the shelter to nurse Layton. When they returned before lunchtime, they gladly found Layton sitting up in bed.

"Well, there's something we're glad to see."

Vance sat down beside Layton. In turn, he smiled and chuckled. This caused the other three to smile and laugh a little too.

"He began to do much better after breakfast this morning. Right after you two left, he sat up and asked where we were. I told him you two were out trying to get more information on that matter."

"Yes, and we do have some news for both of you. We're in the year 1988 and a place called Bellevue."

Rizette and Layton seemed very interested when Vance said this.

"1988... Wow, that's much better than the last two sequences."

Oray felt encouraged by Layton's participation in the discussion. He smiled at Vance, where Layton couldn't see him. Vance winked slyly at Oray and Rizette when he saw Oray smile. This caused them all to stifle their laughter a little. They wanted Layton to continue but could barely contain the joy of seeing him feeling better.

"So, what's the plan, or have we not got to that yet?"

"Well..." Vance and Oray both started to speak at the same time.

"Go ahead, Vance."

"Well, we thought this is probably the best place so far that we can try to blend in. The technology will be of little use, but who knows where we could land if we move to another sequence. We also feel if we can get an operation base somehow, there might be something in this sequence we can use to help our situation."

Oray then spoke as if continuing on Vance's statement.

"At the very least, this seems to be a good sequence to get some rest and recover from the last few days."

Layton thought for a few seconds. "That sounds like a great plan." He then leaned back and put his arms behind his head. "I guess I can just take it easy for the next few days then." He smiled very broadly, and the others laughed.

"You better think again, buddy. There'll be no slackers in this unit."

Vance chuckled after saying this and slapped Layton's leg.

"Good morning, everyone. I heard some laughter over here. Is your friend doing better?"

"Good morning, Mark Stevens," Rizette smiled and greeted Mark first. The others also smiled and greeted him after her.

Vance pointed his hand to Layton.

"Mark Stevens, this is Layton. You kind of met him last night."

Mark put his hand out for Layton to shake.

"Nice to meet you, Layton, and you can just call me Mark."

"All right, Mark. I'm sorry I wasn't in a better condition to meet you last night. From what Rizette has told me, we owe you much."

"Well, don't worry about that right now. In fact, I came over to hopefully help a little more. Do you have no money at all?"

163

When Mark asked this, they all shook their heads to indicate they didn't.

"Okay, I'm going to go talk with a friend of mine who works at a charity thrift store. Under your circumstances, I feel sure I can get some vouchers for you. You can use those vouchers to get some clothes and other things you might need. The clothes will be used, but they're all cleaned well before being put up for sale. Would you be all right with something like this?"

"Anything will be a great help right now, Mark Stevens."

When Oray said this, Mark grimaced a little.

"Okay, great. And I'll tell you what. How about if all of you just call me Mark?"

They all nodded in agreement, and Mark smiled and left to get the vouchers.

For the next several days, Layton continued to improve, though he still tired easily. The four used the vouchers and did some shopping for clothes. When they returned to the shelter, Mark appeared somewhat surprised and even commented on the unique fashion combinations they'd chosen, such as parachute pants mixed with dress shirts and cowboy hats. Rizette also caught his attention with a pair of pink short-shorts and a green halter top. He continued to be a great help to them, however, and though he seemed to notice their peculiarities, he never said much about it.

After a week, Vance and Oray felt confident enough to attempt securing employment. Mark directed them to the employment office, and after breakfast, they walked the ten blocks with a mission on their mind.

"Number fifty-five." The woman at the desk called out the number of the ticket Oray held in his hand. He glanced down at the small paper ticket and then over to Vance. Vance nodded in a manner to show support, and Oray stood up and walked to the desk.

"I need your paperwork, hon." The woman glanced across the desk at Oray. He seemed puzzled and then handed her the small piece of paper with the number on it. She stared oddly at the small paper in her hand. She then looked at Oray as if he were sick or something.

"No, hon, I need the application forms. You should have filled them out before I called your number. The instructions and applications are over there by the tickets."

Oray glanced to where the woman pointed and then replied.

"I'm sorry; I'm new to this process." He tried to sound confident but uninformed.

The woman looked him over, and as she realized he was completely fashion ignorant, she appeared to have a little compassion for him.

"Yes, well, you can fill it out quickly right here, I suppose." She handed several pieces of paper to him and a pen with a cap on it.

Oray picked the pen up and examined it as if looking for an on switch. The style of the pen with the cap resembled something Oray had never seen.

The woman behind the desk put her chin on her folded fist and sat watching him as she might a child attempting to use a complicated tool.

He pointed the pen at the paper and pushed the clip as if it were the button to activate it as he would his diver tool. When nothing happened, he looked at the woman with an expression of confusion. For several seconds the woman simply stared at Oray. Then she slowly put her hand down on the desk.

"Are you trying to tell me you can't write?"

Oray now expressed embarrassment. Considering he had no idea how to make the writing device function, he tried to go with her assumption to minimize the damage.

"I ahh, I guess so."

The woman expressed a little frustration as she retrieved the pen and paper. She exhaled rather dramatically as she put the paperwork back into its spot. She turned back to Oray again as if checking one last time for some cruel joke he may be playing on her. When she saw that he still had the confused expression, she spoke again.

"I think I have just the job for you. I'll draw you a map to find the place. Can you read a simple map?" Oray nodded yes. "All right, this company works with people like you. I hope you don't mind getting a little dirty."

She then took a piece of paper and began drawing a map.

"Thank you, Madam. I am very grateful for your assistance." When he said this, the woman raised her eyes to him briefly but never raised her head from the task of map drawing. Then Oray thought of something.

"I don't want to be a burden, but my friend over there." Oray leaned back and pointed at Vance, who wore parachute pants with a tie-dyed t-shirt under a suit jacket. On his head, he wore a straw cowboy hat.

"I don't think he can write either. Could you get him a job also?"

The woman stared at Vance for a few seconds to be sure she was seeing what she thought she was seeing. Then she looked back at Oray.

"Yes, I believe they'll take the both of you," she replied with a bit of exasperation, then returned to complete her map and handed it to Oray. "Both of you should be at this address first thing in the morning. Just tell them you were sent there from the employment office."

Later, at the shelter, all four celebrated as much as possible under the circumstances.

"Can you believe this guy? Not only did he get himself a job, he got me one too!" Vance patted Oray on the back. Rizette beamed with pride and kissed him on the cheek. Oray smiled sheepishly and mumbled thanks to them.

The following morning, Vance and Oray left the shelter after breakfast and traveled with excitement to the location on the map.

They arrived at a large building that had a sign indicating it was a poultry processing facility.

Once inside, they were given some protective clothing and gloves. Paperwork was filled out, and then they were led to the processing side of the facility.

"All right, you two new guys, follow me," a large man said after the office person introduced him as their foreman.

They went through several doors and eventually walked into a semi-darkened room where live chickens moved about on the floor. Along the middle of the room ran a moving line with hooks on it. Men were catching chickens and hanging them feet-first on the hooks. The line moved up and out of the room with the chickens hanging from it.

"Just do as these guys are doing. I'll leave you with them this week, and then you'll start coming in on third shift next week." The man then stepped back and waved his arm to them, indicating they should go to work.

Oray and Vance looked at each other in anticipation that one or the other would back out of the job. Realizing their precarious position and that Layton and Rizette were depending on them, neither one moved to escape the job. Both slowly moved forward, and soon, the feathers were flying as they began their chicken-catching careers.

Late that afternoon, the two men wearily shuffled into the shelter. Both sat down in a slumping fashion and had dazed expressions on their faces.

Rizette opened two sodas for them that she'd saved from lunch. "So, how did it go? Was it fun?" After she asked them this, she sat down beside Oray.

Before he could reply, she noticed something white on his collar. Reaching up, she pulled the white thing out of his collar and examined it closely.

Meanwhile, Vance attempted to answer her.

"It was... Well, what would you say it was, Oray?"

Looking at Vance with a dazed expression, Oray tried to continue Vance's statement.

"It was uhm, well it was..."

"Is this a feather?" Rizette then spotted another one sticking out from the front of his shirt. She pulled this one out as well and examined it.

"What exactly are you guys doing?"

Vance and Oray looked at each other as if waiting for the other to explain the chicken-hanging job. Eventually, they explained it to Rizette and Layton. Both laughed a little but then expressed a deep appreciation for their sacrifice to help the team.

As the days went by, the two men dedicated themselves to performing well at the poultry processing company. After several weeks, they were both paid, and Mark helped them locate a small, furnished house to rent. As they stood outside gazing upon the little white home they had just rented, Mark expressed his joy.

"I am so happy for all of you right now. It's moments like this that make my job worthwhile. I think you'll be happy here. It's much closer to your jobs, and though the neighborhood isn't the greatest, it isn't the worst either."

Rizette appeared especially happy that they finally had something more stable. "We sure owe you a lot, Mark. We can't thank you enough."

"Yes, well, your success in getting a place of your own is thanks enough. If you ever need anything else, just let me know. I'll do whatever I can to help."

When Layton heard this, he reacted as if a thought had come to his mind. "There is one thing I would like to ask you, Mark."

"Sure thing, Layton. What is it?"

"I just wondered. If someone was to forget something and needed to remember it, would there be any type of memory tonic to help him?"

Mark expressed a look of wonder about this question and glanced at the others to confirm Layton was serious. When he noticed they all stood watching him with anticipation for an answer, he reconsidered Layton's question.

"Well, I don't know of any tonic for memory. I think I would see if the library had any books on memory. That might be a good place to start."

"Where would we find this…'library'?"

Mark again examined the four curiously. Then he smiled slightly and said, "I believe there's one within walking distance from here. I'll drive by on the way back to the shelter to find out exactly where it is. I'll come back in a day or two to check on you. I'll let you know about the library then."

They all thanked Mark again and went into the small house. Within a few days, they were settled in, and Mark came by to check on them. He took Rizette and Layton to the library, so they would know where it was. The walk was about ten blocks, but Layton and Rizette felt they could manage it, so he left them to explore the books.

On the way back to the small home, Layton needed to sit at a bench and rest. He and Rizette talked as a car drove by with loud music playing.

"This library will be beneficial to us. Going through the information is much more laborious, but I suspect there is information we can use there, somewhere."

Rizette smiled and agreed with him. She knew how courageous Layton was being. She knew he must certainly realize he was running out of time. He wanted to help them so much, even though he knew by now, there would be little chance of him surviving disembarkation from the virtual zone.

"You're such an asset to our team, Layton. I never would have thought to ask Mark that question. I'm sure you'll find some information to help us." When she told him this, he appeared to be very happy. He smiled and nodded.

"I think I'm ready now."

Rizette helped him up, and they walked the rest of the way home.

A routine began to develop, and after a month, the four were gaining confidence in being able to function in the virtual sequence.

Then, something happened to remind them of their lack of familiarity with the environment.

Early one morning, as Rizette carried a sack of groceries to the front lawn of their small house, a police car pulled up to her and stopped. The driver's window was down, and the police officer in the car spoke to her before she could reach the front door.

"Come over here a minute young lady."

She turned to the police officer. "Did I do something wrong, sir?"

"You just come on over here for a minute."

Rizette sat her bag down on the front porch and walked over to the police car.

"I've been watching you." The patrolman smiled slyly and then pulled his sunglasses down to expose his eyes as if getting a better look at her. "You're new around here, aren't you?"

She struggled for a response. "We're uhmm from...Charleston."

"Charleston, I thought you had the look of a Southern Belle."

"Yes, that's what I'm told a lot. I have a Southern bell look." She smiled with obvious effort.

"Yeah, I like to keep my eyes on you as you go to the little store up the road. You know, I could give you a ride if you want?"

Rizette thought maybe he was trying to be nice. She was very concerned about being around a local for very long and particularly a police officer. She said the first thing she could think of.

"Well, I'll ask my husband about it."

When she said this, the policeman's demeanor changed very quickly. He put his sunglasses back up over his eyes.

"Yeah, well, don't bother."

He stared at Rizette for several seconds with suspicion.

"Are you and your friends doing drugs?"

She didn't know what to say. She stammered nervously and struggled for an appropriate answer. "We....er...ahh."

"Yeah, well, I'm watching all of you close, little lady. You can tell your husband that." The policeman then put the car into gear and quickly drove away.

When Rizette picked her bag of groceries up and went into the house, she found Oray, Vance, and Layton all standing close to the front windows, as if they'd been watching the whole time.

"What did the law enforcer want?" Oray asked as soon as she entered.

She put her bag on the table, then took a breath as if relieved to be out of the stressful situation. Then she ran her fingers into her hair and kept her hand on top of her head briefly before bringing it down.

"He said he's watching us closely and asked if we were doing drugs."

The three men considered this a few seconds. Vance walked over to the table and glanced in the bag. Oray rubbed his chin and said, "We can't get into any trouble with the law enforcement. If we get incarcerated for anything, we'll never make it out of here alive. If we're supposed to be doing drugs, then we need to find some and start doing them."

Layton and Vance nodded in agreement. Vance then bit into an apple he'd pulled from the bag and began chewing it while in obvious thought on the matter.

"I wonder where we can get drugs," Layton said.

Vance swallowed his bite of apple and, after some thought, replied.

"Maybe the guy next door knows where to get some drugs."

"You mean the one on this side, with the 'Jesus Saves' sign in the yard?" Layton pointed to the left side of the house.

"Yeah, that guy. He probably knows where to get some drugs." Vance then took another bite of the apple. Oray listened to the conversation with interest and then turned to Rizette.

"Did the police officer say anything else? Anything about how many or what type we should be doing?"

Rizette went to the bag of groceries and began pulling the items out one at a time and sitting them on the table.

"Not really."

The others now appeared to give this new information some thought.

Finally, Oray spoke. "Layton, could you find out anything about these 'drugs' at that library you've been going to?"

"Possibly. There are some information sheets they call 'newspapers' that list the daily events. They're the large papers like the one we saw in that 1876 sequence. There may be something in those. I'll check tomorrow when we go."

Later that afternoon, as Vance and Oray prepared for work, Vance noticed their neighbor outside and in the front yard.

"Hey, there's that guy out front. Let's go see if he knows where to find some drugs."

Oray and Layton eagerly stood up from the table and moved over to the window.

"All right, but let's be careful. We don't know much about the situation." Oray replied as he eyed the man from the window.

The three men walked over to the man who stood on a small step ladder adjusting the swing on his front porch.

He glanced down at the three men who now stood watching him.

"Can I help you?"

Now, the three glanced at each other as if wondering which one would do the talking. Then Oray spoke.

"Well, uhm, we heard something about people around here doing 'drugs,' and we just thought maybe you could offer some advice?"

The man stepped down from the ladder and expressed concern.

172

"People doing drugs, this is serious. You should tell me more about it. I can help you take the appropriate steps after we get the information together."

The three looked at each other as if even more confused than before. Then Vance stepped into the conversation rather awkwardly.

"We just wondered if you knew who the people were. Maybe you could tell us what drugs people should be doing? I mean the people who are supposed to do drugs."

Their neighbor stared at them strangely. "Are you guys doing drugs now?"

All three appeared nervous and again seemed to struggle for a response. Finally, Layton asked with some reservation.

"Should we be?"

The man now looked a bit angry.

"Is this some sort of joke? If it is, you should rethink your attempts at humor. I don't play games when it comes to people doing drugs in my neighborhood. Drugs kill people and are bad news altogether. If I find out that you are doing drugs, I will call the law on you. Don't think for a second I won't."

The actual situation became very clear to the three men now.

"Oh, no, sir, we're just joking, sir. We would never do drugs," Oray replied quickly.

"No. We just thought you might like a good laugh…sir." Vance also tried to contain the situation.

Disgusted, the man shook his head as the three smiled sheepishly and began backing out of his yard.

"That's not the least bit funny. You three need to rethink your idea of a joke."

"Oh yes, sir. We'll do that and right away, sir," Layton said.

"Good day to you, sir." Vance waved as they reached their yard. The other two also waved, and then they quickly went into the house and shut the door.

CHAPTER NINE:

ACCESSING THE UNKNOWN

"I've got something!" Rizette helped Layton through the front door. Oray and Vance were sitting at the table drinking coffee.

"We were just wondering if you two would make it back before we went to work," Oray said though he was more concerned about not getting to see Rizette before they left.

"So, what do you have for us, Layton?" Vance asked and then tipped his coffee up to take a drink.

Layton held a book up as he stood inside the doorway. He then raised a hand to indicate he needed to catch his breath.

"It must be something important. He wouldn't stop at our usual resting spot. He insisted on making it here before the two of you left for work." Rizette then led him to a chair as he labored to catch his breath.

"I believe I've found a way to retrieve the second access word from Oray's memory." Layton paused again to breathe but held up the book again, indicating the information to be inside.

Oray expressed a little fear.

"If it has anything to do with drinking a potion or tonic of some sort, count me out. That last attempt at memory retrieval almost killed me."

"No potions, no tonics, but I need to read more about it. If it's what it appears to be and works, there should be no pain whatsoever involved."

Oray relaxed a little, finished his coffee, and sat the cup down. "That sounds promising. You find out more about it tonight, and we'll talk about it tomorrow." Oray then went over to Rizette and gave her a quick hug and kiss.

He then went to the backroom to get dressed for work. Vance also turned his coffee up to finish it. He then held his arms open to Rizette as if she might come over to give him a hug and a kiss.

"You better get out of here!" She picked up a rag from the table and threw it at him.

Vance laughed and headed to a backroom to also get ready for work.

The next morning, Layton was sitting at the table with his book and a cup of coffee.

"You haven't been up all night, have you?" Vance sat his lunch box and other work items on a chair by the door.

"No, I wanted to talk with the two of you, so I got up early. This is very exciting; you both need to look at this."

Oray also sat his work things on the chair, and they both took a seat at the table with Layton.

"It's called hypnosis. It seems to be something akin to the lost potions and rituals you spoke of Vance, but this appears much more promising than anything I've found so far. Look at this."

He turned the book to where they could see a picture.

"This man is called a hypnotist. You see the man lying there. He is what's called 'under hypnosis.' And you see this little device here." He pointed at a small black box on a table beside the man. "That is a recording device. It's recording memories the man couldn't recall ordinarily. But while under hypnosis, he's able to recall those memories, and they're recording them as he speaks."

Oray pulled the book over and examined it with care.

"So, are you sure there's no potion drinking or poking with needles and such?"

"Yes, you don't have to worry about that. There isn't anything to drink or any poking involved."

Rizette came into the kitchen in one of Oray's t-shirts. She yawned and put her hand on her husband's shoulder. She examined the book a little as Oray looked at it.

She then asked sleepily, "Is there anyone else wanting some coffee?"

All three raised their hands without looking up.

"Great. Make me a cup too while you're at it," she then went into the small living room and lay down on the couch.

Realizing they'd been outfoxed, the guys watched her briefly as she got comfortable. Then, they looked at each other, hoping one would volunteer to make the coffee.

The following weekend, Rizette, Vance, and Oray strolled to the shelter where they had initially stayed.

"You ask him." Oray tried to enlist Rizette as they walked up to the outside of the shelter with a small cassette recorder.

"Why should I ask him?"

"Well, he uhm, he really likes you, and I'm certain he would be glad to tell you about the device." Oray attempted to sound sincere as they stood outside the doorway.

She frowned a bit and then looked at the two men. Both stood watching her anxiously.

After a close examination of the two, her eyes expressed surprise.

"You don't want Mark to find out that you know nothing about this recording device!"

Now they seemed to turn their attention away from her as they realized she'd figured the situation out.

"Well, Riz, it's just that…" Vance tried to explain and struggled.

Oray stepped in. "You see Riz, it's just that men during this period are supposed to know such things."

Now Oray and Vance both got excited about this point and tried to work it even more.

"You know, Riz, Mark might get suspicious," Oray explained.

"It's about keeping our cover safe," Vance added, and both men nodded and agreed.

She stood watching them in disbelief while they said these things and struggled in obvious embarrassment.

After a little more elaboration on the matter, they both watched her as if hoping she had bought the flimsy reasoning. For a few seconds, silence prevailed as the three stared at each other.

Then, a smile broke out over Rizette's face, and she shook her head. Then she took the recording device from Oray's hand.

"I don't believe you guys. What a couple of wimps!"

Now the two men looked at each other as neither of them knew what "wimp" meant.

Rizette opened the shelter door and walked inside with the small device in hand.

Oray followed behind closely.

"Hey, just what is this 'wimp' thing you just called us?"

She laughed a little as they moved towards Mark. She raised the palm of her hand to him, indicating she didn't plan to answer.

The two men glanced at each other and shrugged their shoulders as they realized Riz had them right where she wanted them.

"Mark Stevens."

"Hey, hello. I've been meaning to come over and visit you sometime. I've just been busy." He clipped his pen onto his clipboard and turned to give them his full attention.

"Oh, well, that's all right. Oray and Vance have been working a lot. We thought we would come by and see you."

The two men stood behind Rizette as children might stand behind a mother.

"So, how is Layton doing?" Mark asked with concern.

"He's doing better. He just gets tired easily. He stayed at the house but said to tell you hello."

"Okay, well, tell him hello for me."

They stood looking at each other for a few long seconds. Mark struggled to find something to say, and Rizette just smiled and fidgeted a bit.

"So, uhm, is there anything in particular you needed, or is this just a social visit?"

"Uh, well, you see, I was wondering about something," she said and then turned her head slightly towards Oray and Vance with a little smirk, indicating she wasn't afraid, and then continued.

"I just can't seem to get this recording device to function." She held the small cassette player up to Mark.

Once again, a strange, puzzled expression came over Mark's face as he took the cassette player from her hands. He then looked at Vance and Oray, who still stood behind Rizette, watching with keen interest.

"Hmm, well, let's take a look at it." He punched several buttons and looked through the small window to see if anything was working.

"We just bought it this morning," Rizette said as she watched Mark examine it.

"I see the problem. There are no batteries in it."

"Batteries?" all three repeated in unison.

"Yes, batteries." He showed them the empty battery compartment after opening it up.

"Where can we get batteries?"

Mark rubbed the side of his face in apparent astonishment.

"You can probably get batteries at the same store where you bought the player."

"Oh, great. Thanks." Rizette took the player, and then they all started to leave.

Mark now realized if he didn't speak up, they would likely be back soon.

"Hey, you'll need to get the right size batteries."

The three stopped and turned back around.

"Right size, you mean there's more than one size?" Rizette asked as they began to walk back towards him.

"Yeah, there are a number of different sizes. And do you have a blank cassette?"

"Blank ca... what?"

"No, I didn't think so." Mark smiled and took the player from Rizette's hands. "I'll write the information down for you to give to the store clerk."

He pulled a piece of paper from his clipboard and looked inside the cassette player's battery compartment to see the size of battery needed.

"If you don't mind me asking, what do you need a 'recording device' for?"

Rizette peered over his shoulder as he asked this. Then she casually replied.

"Oray is going to be hypnotized, and we want to record what he says while he's under hypnosis."

Mark stopped writing and seemed to have a little trouble grasping what she'd just said. Then, seeming to recall who he was speaking with replied.

"Oh, I see. Well, you'll certainly want to get that on tape," he then went back to writing down the information.

Then he handed the paper to Rizette. Oray and Vance moved close to her and examined the paper as well.

Mark stood watching this with a slight smile of bewilderment. The three of them then looked back at him, and with thanks and a slight wave, they walked towards the doorway.

Mark ran his fingers through his hair as he wondered about the odd event. Then he shook his head a little and went back to work.

Once they acquired the batteries and tape and made a test run with the recorder to be sure they knew how to use it, Layton located a hypnotist in Bellevue and made an appointment for Oray.

As the day approached, Vance and Oray came in from work one morning to find Layton already awake and at the table with a cup of coffee. He sat staring at the recorder as if in thought. Vance and Oray poured some coffee and sat down with him. After some silence and a few sips of coffee, Vance was the first to speak.

"So, if this works, I suppose all we need to do is locate an advisor."

"I believe I have several possible candidates already," Layton said without much emotion.

"Really?" Oray asked.

"Yes, there's a lawyer a few blocks away, and if he's not it, there's a church a bit farther away."

"Well, it seems you've been doing your share of work as well." Vance then sipped his coffee and examined his friend over the rim of the cup.

Layton tapped a finger on his cup silently and said nothing for a few moments. Oray and Vance sat silent also as they realized he had something on his mind. Finally, Layton appeared to find a starting point for what bothered him.

"I know I don't have much longer. I just want to know who did this to us. But if this works, we may land in the middle of a hostile faction. Our success could also mean our doom. I don't want you and Rizette to risk everything for my sake. I don't have to know who did this to us. You three have a reasonable existence here. I want to be sure I'm not a factor in us leaving here if we do happen to land in a bad spot."

Vance glanced across the table at Oray, who looked back at him for a second but said nothing. He took another drink of coffee. Vance then took the lead after giving the situation some thought.

"There's no way you can't be a factor, Layton. We're a team, and no matter what, we live together or die together until we reach an end to this journey. But, just speaking for myself, even if you hadn't come this far, I would continue if possible. So, if we should land in a bad spot, don't feel that I went only for you."

Oray then spoke.

"I appreciate that you're concerned for us, Layton. I agree with Vance, though. You're a part of this team. Even if you didn't make it this far, we would continue not only to find out who did this to us but to find out who did this to you and Carl as well. We want you to have peace and to have that question that burns inside you answered. But we would try to answer it no matter what. Carl deserved better than he got. You deserve better than you got. We may not make it out of the virtual zone alive, but we may be able to at least confront the ones responsible. Rizette and I have already discussed this, and we wouldn't live peacefully, thinking we may have made it out if we'd not stopped trying. You don't need to worry on our account."

Layton now smiled and expressed that this settled the matter for him. He nodded and then patted them both on the arms. After getting up and pouring another cup of coffee, he sat back down just as Rizette walked in, clearing the sleep from her eyes. She put her arms around Oray's neck and kissed him on the ear. Then she said sleepily.

"Did I miss anything?" The guys chuckled a little but said nothing.

The day slowly arrived for Oray's hypnosis session.

All four walked cautiously into the hypnotist's office. From the various signs around the office, it appeared this man was not only a hypnotist but also a locksmith and notary public, among other things. Soon, the man came from a room behind the counter.

"Hello, one of you must be 'Oray'? Did I pronounce that right?"

"Yes, sir, I'm Oray. You pronounced it right."

"Great, my name is Mike Simpson."

Oray introduced Rizette and the others.

"So, you want to be hypnotized, Oray?"

Rizette now jumped in. "He doesn't have to drink anything, does he?"

"No, not at all. It's really a simple procedure. There have been great strides made recently with hypnosis assisting people who wish to stop smoking or drinking, as well as other undesirable habits. And all without drugs or other substances that have potential side effects. I'm guessing you're here for something along those lines, maybe?"

"Can it help me remember something?"

"Remember something?" Mike appeared a little puzzled and considered the question. "Yes, I'm sure it can. I've not had as much experience with that type of thing, but I'm sure there is a chance of success. How long ago was the thing or event you wish to remember?"

The four of them sort of huddled together and spoke with hushed voices. Mike could hear very little but noticed they spoke as if they had traveled somewhere. One would mention something, and then the other would add to that, and after a minute or two of this Oray turned back to Mike.

"Around six or seven months ago, I think, there are some blurry things in between now and then, so I'm not absolutely for certain."

Mike expressed an odd face as if a little confused. But realizing Oray was quite serious, he replied.

"That's all right, as long as we're not talking about twenty years or more. You may need someone more skilled for that length of time. But you must realize I can't guarantee anything. This is something that has had success as well as failure in these situations. As long as you understand this, we can proceed."

"We understand," Vance said and then, lifting the small recorder, asked, "Can we record what he says?"

"I suppose so if it's all right with Oray. You'll need to be quiet during the process, though."

Oray assured Mike he wanted the others to be present. They paid Mike for the service as he stated it would have to be cash in advance. Mike then wrote down all the questions and information regarding the memories Oray wished to have retrieved. After confirming his notes back to Oray, he led them to the backroom and turned the lights down. Oray was seated in a half-reclining position, and once Vance had started the recorder, the procedure began.

Rizette, Vance, and Layton watched with interest as Mike slowly and methodically ushered Oray into a hypnotic state. He then asked Oray to repeat the oath and access information Riley gave him, word for word.

Oray slowly and methodically repeated the information, just as Riley had given it to him.

Now, the other three moved closer, and Mike became a little surprised as all three came creeping up very close to Oray as if the words he spoke meant the difference between life and death.

Vance held the recorder closer and closer as Oray relayed the words Riley spoke and then his own words.

When he got to the second access word and said "Merrimack," the other three looked at each other and lipped the word silently as if it were a golden key they didn't want to lose.

Once Oray had reached a point of mentioning no further diver information, Mike quietly conferred with the other three about whether they had all they needed. Vance whispered they did have all the necessary information, and Mike brought Oray out of the hypnotic state.

"Merrimack," they said as he began sitting up.

"Merrimack, what does that mean?" Oray turned to Mike." What does that mean? It's not in the dictionary. Layton and I went through the M's several times, and I would have recognized it if I'd seen it."

Mike turned the lights up as Oray said this. "Merrimack, you mean you've never heard of the Merrimack?"

183

"No, should I have?"

"Well, the reason it's not in some dictionaries is it's not actually a descriptive word. It's a name. The Monitor and the Merrimack were iron-clad ships during the Civil War. They fought a famous battle with each other that ended in a draw. I'm surprised you've never heard of it."

Sensing they were somewhat exposing their lack of historical knowledge, Layton tried to wrap things up quickly.

"Oh yes, everyone has heard of that battle. I guess the fun is over then. I think we should be going now."

The others quickly picked up on Layton's thoughts and began moving towards the door.

Rizette smiled and shook his hand.

"Thank you, Mike. You've really solved a little mystery for us."

Then she moved out the door with the others as Mike replied politely, "Yes, you're certainly welcome. Goodbye."

Back at their small house, the four sat at the table listening to the tape.

"There doesn't seem to be any clear indication of who the 'creed' is or what this station actually is either." The others nodded in agreement with Vance's statement.

"Commissioner Redstone appeared very apprehensive when I spoke with him at my aunt's office. The way he spoke, there was a faction challenging his authority over the virtual facility. My aunt also told me he doubled his security. Why would he do that unless there was a dangerous entity in existence?"

The others considered Rizette's information.

"Didn't your aunt say something about the commissioner assuming more control over the facility?" After Oray asked her this, she seemed to recall the information.

184

"Yes, she said he'd been assuming more control over the virtual zone systems. According to the commissioner, this was to help him resolve the situation with those opposing him."

Layton now turned to her.

"Did your aunt ever mention the creed?"

"She never mentioned any creed. The commissioner didn't either. She simply said something was wrong in the virtual zone, and the commissioner had increased his control and security due to the problem. One council member and his family had disappeared, but according to what the commissioner told my aunt and the other council members, this council member left to escape being implicated in a plot against him. The commissioner told me he wouldn't allow subversives to take control of the virtual zone. I think he told me this because he suspected me or possibly Oray and me both of being a part of this subversive faction."

Rizette watched the men as if waiting for a response to this information. They all thought the situation over but didn't appear confident in making any assumptions. Finally, after the silence became almost unbearable, Layton made a comment to ease the tension.

"With the information we have, I would venture to say we don't really have a clue as to what's going on or what we might run into at this 'station' once we get there; if we get there."

The others nodded in affirmation to his comment. Again, they all sat in silence as if a calamity were about to befall them. Then, Oray suddenly clapped his hands together and said in a rather enthusiastic tone. "So, are we leaving today or tomorrow?" This pulled everyone back from the edge of doom, and they laughed. Rizette pushed her husband's shoulder in a gesture of support for his light-hearted move.

"Who wants coffee?" Rizette asked. No one raised their hand. "All right, who wants coffee if I make it?" The three men's hands went up immediately. She laughed and got up to make the coffee.

The next morning, the four of them stopped by the shelter. They stood in their mismatched fashions at the door until Mark noticed them and came over to talk.

"Hey, how are you guys, oh, and gal?" Mark smiled and pointed to Rizette after correcting himself.

The four didn't seem to catch his quirky comment, which left him smiling and chuckling alone. After a tense second of waiting for them to react to his humorous remark, Mark collected himself and became serious as he noticed his visitors appeared to be.

"We've come to tell you goodbye, Mark Stevens." Rizette didn't appear sad when she said this but seemed 'not happy' to Mark. He became even more serious now.

"Goodbye. Where are you going?"

"Away," she said. The three men simply stood behind her and appeared 'not happy.'"

"We want to thank you for all of your assistance."

Mark nodded a little and tried to think of something to help get a location from them.

"Well, I'd like to maybe come and visit all of you some time."

"I'm afraid that's not possible," Oray replied without emotion and continued. "We want you to know, however, that you've been successful in your efforts to assist those in need. You've been more helpful to us than you could ever know, and we're very grateful."

Mark appeared at a loss for anything to say. After a few awkward seconds, he replied. "Thank you. I'm going to miss you all. But I also want you to know that you've made me very happy and I feel successful when I think of the four of you. I'm not sure where you came from or where you're going, but you've made a difference in my life as well."

They all smiled when he said this. Then Rizette hugged him, and the other three all shook his hand. They filed out of the shelter, with Mark sadly watching them leave.

Soon, the four arrived at the parking lot of a lawyer's office that was around five blocks from their small house. As they approached the front door, Layton explained his theory.

"One of the advisors was a preacher in a church. Another was a counselor, which is also known as a lawyer or legal advisor. So, I found the closest of both to where we live. This lawyer is actually a bit closer. But if the doorway isn't here, I suspect it will be at the church a few blocks from here."

"But what about when we move? Wouldn't that change the advisor?"

Layton smiled slightly as if prepared for Vance's question.

"Sure, it would. The advisors will likely change as we move around. I suspect, however, the stipulation is always the advisor closest to Oray or to us. Therefore, I found the closest advisors to where we live. They wouldn't move around, so when we were ready, we had the closest advisor available."

Vance, Oray, and Rizette looked at him with an expression of being impressed. This caused him to smile, and then he marched up the steps to the door with the others following.

Walking through the doorway, they found a young woman at a desk.

"May I help you?"

"We need to speak with the legal advisor." Vance wasted no time.

"Do you have an appointment?"

A tense second passed as they considered what to do. Then Oray spoke. "I believe I might have. I'm Oray 536. I wish to access Merrimack."

When Oray said this, the young woman's face went blank, and she appeared to freeze in place.

"Well, that did something anyway," Vance noted as he waved his hand in front of the woman's face. As he did this, a man in a suit opened a door and walked out of the office that sat behind her desk. He had his head down, examining paperwork.

"Miss Sanders, can you get me the file for..." Raising his head, he immediately noticed the strange appearance of his secretary. "What's going on here? What have you done to Miss Sanders?"

Before the man could say anything else, Oray intervened. "Oray 536, I wish to access Merrimack."

Immediately, the man's face went blank. He turned and walked back into his office. Oray and the others moved around the secretary's desk and followed him.

The man walked up to a large display cabinet. Trophies and various other items were on display, but when the man opened it, light replaced the items, and a virtual doorway took their place.

"Are we ready?" Oray looked at the others to make sure they were all prepared for the unknown ahead of them.

Rizette said. "Yeah," as she stared at the doorway. The others nodded and mouthed affirmation as they peered into the light. They locked arms as before and went through the door.

CHAPTER TEN:

THE GREED AWAKENS

Darkness and silence surrounded the four. When their eyes became accustomed to the dim light, they found themselves in a large vacant area. Far ahead, they could see a single large building with what appeared to be a dome on top and rays of light shining out in all directions.

Layton then noticed a pathway under their feet and pointed it out to the others. They could see the path clearly but couldn't locate the source of light. Oray moved first and walked past the others towards the large building.

Although the building initially seemed far away, the four came to the front after a very short walk.

A large open doorway unexpectedly presented itself before them. Through the doorway, they could see what resembled an old-world train station. There were lit-up shops that looked to be food vendors. Other areas also recalled the long-past days of rail transit.

In the middle of the open area, a fountain of light rather than water displayed a brilliant spectacle; directly above this, a huge ball floated with multicolored rays of light streaming in all directions from the middle. This caused the inside of the overhead dome to light up. As they examined the top of it closer, a multitude of virtual scenes could be viewed, mingled together and playing out across the inside of the dome.

189

The four stood outside the door, peering in cautiously for several seconds before Oray motioned for them to enter. They began to go in when suddenly a man dressed in an old-style uniform appeared directly in front of the four. He said nothing but simply stood before Vance, who would have been the first to enter.

Once they recovered from the initial shock, Oray spoke.

"Try to go around him."

Vance moved to the side, but the man, seeming to slide on air rather than use his feet, continued to block Vance.

Oray moved up and approached the man, prepared to utter the access code when quite unexpectedly, the man in uniform spoke.

"Hello Oray, 536. Welcome to Diver Creed Station."

He became a little startled by this and glanced back at the others with obvious surprise.

He then turned back to the man.

"Do you know me?"

"Of course, I know you; it's my job to know all the divers of the creed. How may I assist you?"

"We wish to access the station."

"I recognize you, Oray 536, but I don't recognize the others with you."

Oray looked back at the other three and then down to the ground as if straining for an answer, then he replied. "They're my assistants. I need them with me."

The man in the uniform expressed a puzzled look but then said, "Please wait. I must confer with the senior officials." He then disappeared as if he had evaporated.

Oray moved closer to the doorway, then moved his hand to the opening, and as it crossed the plane of the entryway, he recognized there was an energy field present. Vance moved up beside him and tried to put his hand through the doorway, but his hand became blocked by the energy field.

"If we can't get in, I guess it's the end of the road for us," Vance said quietly so Rizette and Layton wouldn't hear.

"There's still hope, as long as I can get in. Maybe if I can access a control panel inside. I can do something."

Vance grunted an affirmation as he inspected the energy field blocking his entry.

Suddenly, the man in uniform appeared in front of them again.

"Your assistants may utilize the basic facilities. However, they may not access any of the higher-level facilities. Are you in agreement with this?"

Oray glanced at Vance with a flash of excitement and replied. "Yes, I'm in agreement."

"Very well then. You may proceed, along with your assistants."

The man in uniform then evaporated again from the doorway. Oray moved through the door. Vance, Rizette, and Layton followed behind him.

Inside the massive building, the four became immediately impressed by the elaborate and luxurious decor. Around the walls were eateries and rooms containing entertainment services. As they made their way around, Rizette peered with curiosity into one of the doorways. The well-lit sign above it read "Rest Stop." Inside, she saw clean beds in small individual compartments.

Continuing, they came across shower rooms and more eateries of various old-world cultural cuisine.

"So many places to eat and no one to take our order," Oray commented, as there was no one to be one seen behind the counters of the eateries.

"Can we just sit at the table for a few moments? I'm afraid I need a little break." Layton appeared tired and weak.

"Yeah, let's rest a few minutes," Vance said and sat down at a table in front of a small 'Greek Cuisine' eatery.

Immediately after the four sat down, a man in a white uniform appeared from seemingly nowhere.

"May I take your order, or would you like to hear our specials of the day first?"

All four of them examined this man with surprise and a little shock. Then Rizette glanced at the others and replied. "Let's hear the specials, please."

The man in the white uniform proceeded to relay the specials to the four of them, after which they each ordered.

Within minutes of ordering, the waiter brought their food out. It was the best food they could recall eating.

"So, what do you think this place is? It's certainly not what I expected." Vance seemed to be directing his question to Oray but also looked at Rizette and Layton.

They all gazed around the vast facility. They saw no one, yet everything at the station appeared to be in a state of readiness.

"It's all very strange, isn't it?" Rizette seemed to speak to relieve the tension in the air. "I mean, there's no one here. But from the way it looks, everything is ready for, well, a lot of people to suddenly show up."

The others continued to study the station as she said this.

Oray then commented. "I wonder if the station is just some leftover facility from the old world. Maybe there used to be activity here for some reason, but now it's just an idle relic of a bygone day."

Vance nodded in agreement. "That could be. As far as virtual sequences go, this place is taking up no more than a micro fragment of space on a massive file somewhere. If this creed had some agenda in the old world, it could be long gone and forgotten. The station, however, could just be floating endlessly in a misplaced file in cyberspace."

The small group left the eatery and walked on, investigating the various facilities along the way. Rizette was amazed when she used a lady's restroom and found a female attendant by the door on her way out. She held a towel and various perfumes on a tray. Rizette sprayed one on her and laughed a little at this unusual luxury.

"Wow, you smell nice!" Oray immediately noticed the perfume when his wife approached.

"Yeah, there was no one at the door when I walked in. But when I came out, there was an attendant with a towel and perfumes on a tray." Rizette glanced back as she said this and realized the female attendant no longer stood at the door.

"We need to find a control center. Surely there's a control panel or data center here somewhere." Oray scanned the area as he said this.

"We've only covered half the station. Let's keep going. We can take a break when Layton needs to." Vance then glanced back at Layton, who was already falling back and seemed to be struggling to keep up.

Oray also glanced back to Layton, who was now being assisted by Rizette

"That sounds good. I don't think we'll have any problems with food or a place to sleep. We can go until we find a data center of some type, or we get tired of searching."

As they came to the far end of the station, there was a large open area resembling a large doorway, except there was no actual door. Instead, there was only thick darkness. The four stood and stared into the dense emptiness for several seconds. Then Vance asked.

"Do we want to go in there?"

Rizette quickly answered him. "No, we don't want to go in there!"

He looked at her and smiled a little. They continued past the dark doorway and soon came upon a spacious and well-lit control center.

"Now, this is exactly what we've been looking for." Oray held his hands out towards the find. He then quickly walked into the data control room. The others began to follow him into the room.

Suddenly, an energy field materialized, keeping Oray inside the room and the others outside. When Oray noticed the others were not behind him, he turned and tried to go back out but couldn't pass through the energy field. He pounded on the invisible barrier to get back through. When Rizette realized the field separated them, she screamed out and landed against the field, also pounding it with her hands.

"Oray!" she struck the blocked entryway again and again. Oray pounded on his side. They yelled to each other, but no sounds penetrated the field.

Then, Vance stepped back from the entrance. Rizette noticed what Vance had seen, and she also stepped back a little. Two men in gray suits had materialized behind Oray. They came closer to him.

Oray noticed she and Vance were looking at something behind him. He turned and faced the two men. He then appeared to be speaking with them.

In vain, Rizette again struck the energy field with her hands. Oray turned to her briefly. His eyes expressed fear of something unknown. One of the men then looked at Rizette. He raised his hand out towards her. The energy field darkened instantly.

"No, Oray, Oray...!" Rizette began to cry as she leaned against the darkened barrier. She stepped back as tears rolled down her cheeks. Vance moved closer and stood beside her.

She continued to stare at the darkened doorway but asked softly, "What's happening, Vance?"

He also stared at the darkened energy field for several seconds as if it might become clear again. Then he replied in a hushed voice, "I wish I knew."

Rizette stepped back a few more steps. She sat down with her legs crossed and watched the door intently. Vance sat down as well. Behind them, Layton had already almost lain down from exhaustion.

The minutes ticked by slowly. Then hours began to pass by. Vance retrieved two plates of food for Rizette and Layton. Then he helped

Layton to a rest area to get some sleep. Still, Rizette refused to leave the darkened door. After getting Layton situated, Vance took a pillow and blanket to Rizette. She had already fallen asleep in a sitting position. He nudged her and showed her the blanket and pillow. She lay down with them and slept for a while.

Time seemed to stand still. Nothing moved in the vast station other than the constant light fountain in the middle that appeared to never cease its display.

Rizette would lay back occasionally to watch the glimpses of virtual scenes streaming across the massive dome. What seemed to be a week passed by, but she realized it was around two days.

Vance brought her food, and other than an occasional bathroom break, she stayed in front of the doorway. Then, when she was beginning to worry Oray would never return, the door cleared and opened suddenly.

Rizette sat up.

"Vance. Vance...."

He came over quickly just as the two men in gray suits materialized and walked towards them. Then Oray materialized behind them. Rizette let out a sigh of relief, but then her heart almost stopped. Oray wore a gray suit identical to the two men in front of him.

She stood up now and wanted to run to her husband. She made an involuntary whining sound as she was torn between relief and fear. Vance moved over in front of her as the men came closer. She stepped to the side of him to see her husband.

A tear rolled down her cheek as she searched for any sign that Oray was the same man that stepped into the room a few days earlier. The two men stepped right up to Rizette and Vance. Oray then stepped between them and stood in the middle.

"Oray...?" she almost whispered his name as she moved around Vance and towards him. Now he realized what his wife was thinking.

He held out his arms to her. She immediately began to cry with joy as she landed in his arms. Vance also relaxed now.

Once Rizette had calmed down, Oray pointed to the two men one at a time and introduced them.

"These men are the senior officials. They are, in fact, the founders of the diver creed. This is Jackson, and this is Hugh."

The men smiled and shook hands with Rizette and Vance, calling them by name as they did so. Then Jackson spoke.

"Actually, we're the virtual representations of Jackson and Hugh. However, the real Jackson and Hugh put great effort into our creation and development. I believe you'll find us far superior to any NLP in the virtual zone."

Rizette looked at her husband. "What is this place? And what is the diver creed?"

"I think Jackson and Hugh can explain everything much more efficiently than I could." After he said this, he turned to Jackson on his right, indicating Jackson should speak. Jackson, in turn, leaned forward to glance across to Hugh.

"Would you like to take this, Hugh?"

Hugh smiled, "Sure, I would be delighted." He then began walking towards the large dark doorway they'd been so wary of several days earlier. They began to follow him when suddenly Vance stopped.

"Wait, we need to get Layton. He's at the rest area."

"If you'll go to the rest area, I'll have an assistant meet you there."

When Jackson said this, Vance nodded with a little uncertainty.

But, as Vance arrived at the rest area, he saw what appeared to be a young, attractive female nurse outside the doorway. She had a wheelchair with her, and she smiled when he approached.

"I'm here to assist with Mr. Layton, sir."

Vance smiled back at her and replied, "Thank you, miss. He's in here." She followed him in, and soon they had a somewhat surprised Layton in the chair and on the way back to the others.

When they reached the others, Layton asked in a weak tone, "Who are they?"

"Hello, Layton. My name is Jackson, and this is Hugh. We're the founders of the diver creed."

"What is the diver creed?" Layton asked.

"Hugh and I are going to explain everything. We wanted to be sure you were here before anything else proceeded."

"Thank you," Layton replied. He appeared delighted about this, though obviously weak.

They began to move into the large, darkened doorway, and as they did, everything began to light up. All around them, the environment shifted and shaped itself until they found themselves at the front of the virtual facility. It wasn't the old, faded, and weather-worn facility they were familiar with, however. This was a brand-new facility with bright white exterior and personnel in clean uniforms walking about busily. This was obviously the way the virtual facility appeared when it was still new.

"We've spent the last few days with Oray to gain a clear perspective on the current situation." As Hugh spoke, they followed him around the vibrant facility. He walked slowly, and those listening to him marveled at the sights as he explained the things they had wondered about.

"In 2075, the tech company Virtuacorp had the ability to assemble a virtual facility such as this one. However, it didn't have the capital to build such a facility. It put together small units for virtual activities but nothing like the facility it really wanted to create.

"The defense department also wanted a virtual facility to train its military personnel. A facility such as this would cut the costs of training in half. But due to numerous police actions and mini wars around the world, it didn't have the funds to buy the technology for such a facility. The result would eventually be a partnership between a conglomerate of private tech companies that would become known as Virtua-Gauge Corporation and the defense department. After five years of construction, the facility became a reality.

"This is the virtual facility as Jackson, and I knew it. The facility was completed in early 2080. The first of multiple virtual sequence tests took place by mid-2080, and by the end of that year, 773 pods were in full operation. At the peak of operations, over 3,400 pods were in operation. The facility had a total of 3,850 pods available at that time."

As Hugh said this, the scenes around them changed to the long rows of pod compartments. Though recognizable, the new appearance of the pods was quite impressive. Rizette glanced into one of the compartments to view the sight of a brand-new, open pod.

"The main database contains files from world libraries as well as military databases and massive private information collections. The facility has the capacity to create virtual sequences from the dawn of man all the way up to the day it was shut down and the facility placed into hibernation mode.

"Incidentally, the catalog that is being used by Commissioner Redstone is actually a very small introduction catalog. It would be considered something of an advertisement in comparison to the actual capacity of this facility. Basically, only about 3% of the facility's database for virtual sequence creation is being utilized at this time."

Vance appeared shocked by this statement, "Only 3% of the database available? Why would the commissioner only open 3% of the available sequences?"

Now Jackson spoke to answer Vance. "From our investigation with Oray over the last several days, it seems when Commissioner Redstone reactivated the facility, he didn't have the primary access codes. He only had several of the secondary maintenance codes. Basically, the commissioner entered the data system through a back door or window so-to-speak. Therefore, there was only a very limited amount of virtual sequence material available."

Hugh picked up where Jackson left off.

"The designers of the system began to realize some of its weaknesses in early 2081. They'd intentionally placed a gap between the virtual world and the real world for security reasons. Anytime you have artificial intelligence and basic emotional capacities united, there's a risk. Imagine if you will 2,000 pods full of diplomats, government officials, and high-ranking officers. If the non-living personnel were to decide they wanted more from their existence and revolted, they could possibly take these people hostage in the virtual zone, and of course, chaos would be the result.

"So, the gap, or as divers would begin to call it 'the lower level,' was put into place as a barrier for any potential danger from the NLPs. This security measure effectively made many key maintenance and utility actions impossible for the NLPs. Only actual living people could perform these key functions.

"As time went by and the virtual zone ramped up to full speed, the massive amount of information being processed began to produce the enormous number of 'glitches' that resulted from such a system.

"Initially, there were only a few technicians for this aspect of the system. These were simply called 'lower-level maintenance personnel.' Then the reality of the situation slowly demanded a small army of these specialized technicians, and as time went by, they were simply called divers."

As Hugh said these things, the scenes around them changed to the lower levels that Oray, Vance, and Layton were familiar with. Rizette gazed around with interest as she had never seen the lower levels.

"The problem for the divers surfaced as more and more became lost in the vast virtual spectrum. The military had control over maintenance personnel. But the divers were not military. They were private sector technicians. The military officials had little concern for what they felt to be a few divers becoming drifters in the system. The military's thoughts were, 'Why worry about a few private sector technicians when thousands of their soldiers were dying in battlefields every day.'

"When a diver became a drifter, the military commanders would simply move the pod to an isolated holding area and forget about them. A new diver would be given that diver's job, and nothing would be done to retrieve the lost diver."

As he spoke of these things, the scenes around them shifted to personnel in uniforms unhooking a pod. Then they rolled the pod out of the small compartment, and a new one came rolling in behind it. As the group continued to walk, the scenes again changed to show the military personnel hooking the pod up in a dimly lit room, and in this room were hundreds of other pods along the walls. They realized these pods must be divers who were lost in the virtual zone and had become drifters.

"As senior divers, Jackson and I organized a petition for locating and retrieving the lost divers. We also requested a method be devised for divers to exit the system should they become drifters. Virtua-Gauge, however, passed the responsibility on to the military. Their reasoning was that the military held authority over the maintenance side of the facility. The military, in turn, passed the problem back to Virtua-Gauge. Their reasoning was that the system itself was the problem. They suggested Virtua-Gauge finance a revamp of the system to correct an obvious fault. In the end, both sides refused to do anything for the divers.

"Jackson and I refused to give up. By this time, I'd moved into a control position, but after years of diver work, I knew the hazards well.

"My best friend, Jackson, on the other hand, continued to face these dangers almost daily. With no help from management, we evaluated our options. The solution came like a bolt of lightning one evening as we had a beer and watched a game at a local sports bar.

"During a halftime show, Jackson casually made the statement, 'Since we're getting no help from management and no help from the military officials, we should have the right to create a solution ourselves.' Suddenly, we realized what we must do. We smiled at each other, and at that instant, I believe the diver creed came into being.

"With myself in a control position and Jackson in a diver position, we knew the way lay clear to implement a solution. I could put the information in place on the control side, and Jackson could perform the necessary actions within the lower level. We began with a simple plan to establish an escape route should Jackson become lost in the virtual zone. In time, this would develop into the station. Then, our aspirations began to grow, and we realized we should establish a method to retrieve those lost in the virtual zone and provide basic preventative measures to help minimize the risks of becoming drifters. This eventually became the security branch of the creed."

As they listened to Hugh, all the scenes from the creation of the creed played out around them. The station was a simple multi-door establishment and was then built up as they walked along. Hugh continued as the scenes caught up to the place he was speaking of.

"As we built the diver creed facilities inside the virtual zone, Jackson and I realized we could and should bring more divers in. We would need to screen them first. Jackson thought of a security method in which, if any diver was being screened and turned on us, all information he gave would appear as glitches when investigated. However, this seldom occurred, as almost all the divers were delighted to find a way to be secure in the virtual zone.

"During the height of operations at this facility, we had over three hundred divers in the creed. These divers worked on the facilities in the lower level for thirty minutes here and an hour there until the station you see now was constructed.

"Next, we began retrieving those divers who'd become drifters. Some had already passed the point of retrieval. We would place those in a comfortable environment when we could locate them.

"All of the diver creed functions were performed without the military or Virtua-Gauges' knowledge. We soon realized the creed had more power and control over the virtual zone than the military and Virtua-Gauge combined.

"With our newfound power and control over the facility, we decided we must take a responsible approach. The strict code we had loosely been calling the 'creed' was at that time made our official guideline, and members were required to follow it. Jackson then moved the security division into a more proactive function. During the ramp-up of the security division, Jackson discovered many military personnel, as well as Virtua-Gauge officials, who were conducting criminal activities and abusing the virtual zone.

"Through these abuses, individual persons were being sacrificed or disposed of in the virtual zone. If an official wanted to eliminate someone who opposed him or her, the official could pay a price, and that person would become a drifter in the system at some point. We were shocked to discover the corruption to be quite rampant.

"After ten years in operation, the creed felt strong enough to implement a form of defense and justice within the virtual zone that would affect all aspects of the facility yet keep the creed a secret. The system collected information and data concerning the abuses of military and Virtua-Gauge officials.

"When enough data had been collected, a board of senior divers would evaluate the charges against the person or persons. Then, if the case was clearly an abuse of power, a senior diver would put in motion a process that would dump a small but critical piece of information into the hands of an officer or other official who had the ability to prosecute the abusive individual. With a key piece of information in hand, the official would be able to follow a trail to the entire case against the individual. This all appeared to be from an accident or misstep on the guilty party's part. For example, the guilty person may appear to have accidentally placed someone on a message by mistake or a key piece of information dumped into an assistant's file by mistake. However, the creed would be the conduit through which the information would find its way into the right hands.

"Our virtual control system became so efficient at developing unique methods for passing this critical information into the right hands that the diver creed remained completely unknown to all but the creed itself.

"We not only defended the divers; we, in fact, were the dominant regulators of the facility. Almost nothing happened in the virtual zone that we didn't have knowledge of. I am proud to say the diver creed held its prestigious position with pride and honor throughout its existence. That existence, however, would come to an end along with the rest of the facility in 2106.

"By 2105, we had no doubt the facility would be put into hibernation mode. The military had left a contingent of soldiers and officers to defend its interest in the facility but otherwise had left us almost defenseless.

"The wars and chaos had entered into the country with a destructive force unseen before. Diseases now moved unchecked throughout the states. Mass deaths began to sweep over the land. The fallout from weapons also began to kill thousands upon thousands. Being in the central part of the country where we were, the facility remained secure longer than many other areas. Yet, we could see the fall coming. Soon, plans were put into place, and the work of securing and shutting down the facility began in earnest.

"The creed didn't waste this time either. The general idea by the military and Virtua-Gauge was to put the facility into hibernation mode, then head to the high grounds. In the high mountains, we could set up a defensive position and hopefully ride out the chaos. Afterward, the thought was to return to the facility and resume operations at some point.

"To those of us in the creed, this seemed optimistic but doubtful. As far as the creed itself was concerned, we saw little hope of ever returning to the facility. We decided at that point to put a plan in place. If anyone survived and the facility returned to operations, we wanted the creed to also have a chance of survival and continuation. At this point, we felt the creed was a critical element in successful operations of the facility."

As he spoke of these things, they moved about the facility and witnessed personnel busily preparing it for the hibernation state. A few military personnel could be seen with weapons guarding the company personnel as they sealed the pod compartments with foam-like material. Other personnel sealed up databases and control centers with weatherproof materials. All around them, people moved with urgency. Hugh then continued.

"The diver creed senior officials decided to implement a dormant security program. We felt that if the facility should ever be restarted, it would eventually need divers. Also, there would be the potential for abuse and corruption, as we had already experienced. The parameters of the original creed design couldn't be circumvented, though. By this, I mean, an actual living diver would be necessary to engage any security enforcement. This was the most challenging hurdle we had to work through.

"The proposition that senior officials presented to the creed, and was eventually voted on and implemented, was a step-by-step process. First, after a restart of the facilities at some point in the future, a trigger of abuse must occur within the system. With this action, our progressive security program would become active."

Now, the group viewed a fully active Diver Creed Station with members moving to and fro. Divers were obviously preparing for the shutdown. In another scene, the divers were in line and appeared to be voting on the progressive security system. Another scene presented

Jackson at a large display, entering data with Hugh and several other senior divers standing behind him as if assisting.

Hugh continued.

"Next, the future diver must display personal integrity to be considered a candidate for a reawakened diver creed. Finally, that living diver must agree to the same creed we all agreed to. Once these things had taken place, the new diver would be brought up to speed by Jackson and me. Then the abuse or corruption could be properly dealt with, and a new corps of divers could hopefully be initiated."

At this point, the scenes changed to outside the facility. Jackson, Hugh, and a host of other facility personnel could be seen moving out the gates of the complex. Jackson now spoke as if giving Hugh a break.

"We left the facility in September of 2106. The automated security system that guarded it was placed in sleep mode only to awaken with threats to the outer perimeter. In this state, it was believed the thorium energy packs, along with solar plants powering the security system, would last at least eighty to a hundred years. Then there would also be the strength of the facility itself for potential trespassers to deal with. All in all, we felt the facility itself would remain intact until we or someone returned.

"Unknown to the defense department and VG officials, the creed's progressive security system had also been placed into a dormant state, only to become functional once all the triggers and requirements had been activated.

"For the most part, the facility personnel thought we would be in the high mountains a few years, perhaps five years at maximum. The workers and military thought things would settle down, and the government would regain control. This obviously didn't happen. What took place between the time we left the facility and Commissioner Redstone reactivated it is largely unknown. From the research we've done over the last several days with Oray, it seems probable that

Redstone is a descendant of the military officials who carried the access codes with them into the high mountains.

"From information he's entered into the system over the years, we suspect there was a splitting of the Virtua-Gauge personnel and the military personnel at some point. This may be why Commissioner Redstone returned to the facility with secondary access codes rather than primary ones.

"Regardless of how he came into possession of the access codes, he had at least one that provided initial access to the facility and reactivated it; almost a hundred years after the living Jackson, Hugh, and other divers of the creed fled to the mountains."

At this point, the scenes evaporated, and only a white room remained around them. They stood silent for a few seconds. All of them appeared to be considering what Jackson and Hugh had just revealed to them. Then Layton asked the question they had wanted answered for some time now.

"So, who did this to us? I've been trying to survive long enough to find out who did this to us."

Jackson and Hugh smiled with compassion. They then looked at Oray. He, in turn, looked at them as if to ensure they wanted him to reveal this. Once he was sure, he began to speak.

"The access codes Commissioner Redstone used to reactive the facility were secondary codes, and though he could access certain levels and areas of the facility, he was denied direct access. The codes he possessed were likely of a second-level maintenance officer. As Hugh mentioned earlier, he basically reactivated the system by entering the back door. This is why the selection of virtual sequences has always been very limited, though we never actually realized it. The catalog we use to select virtual sequences was pretty much a brief sales catalog that only held a fraction of the available sequences this facility has to offer."

Oray now began to walk, and the others followed him. As they began to walk again, the scenes began to coincide with what he spoke of.

"Commissioner Redstone was compelled to set up a board of living council members like the officers in place when the facility was in full operation. Since his access codes were not for full access, as he would have liked, he's had to use these board members to slowly authorize him more control of the facility. His problem has been to gain access through the council members and solidify that control without revealing his true intentions.

"The council members have been led to believe Commissioner Redstone wanted a unilateral form of government. But from the information collected by the diver creed security system, he has worked tirelessly to break into the military side of the virtual zone. From everything gathered to this point, Commissioner Redstone wants to train new military personnel to build weapons for this military. That's not necessarily a criminal offense. The crimes have been committed by the commissioner through his endeavors to gain total control over the system.

"Commissioner Redstone is directly responsible for at least six people's deaths over the years. He's trapped them inside the virtual zone, and they all died prematurely. These have been people who threatened to expose his efforts of totalitarian rule or otherwise simply got in his way at some point."

When Oray said this, Layton gazed out into an open area of the scenes they viewed. He seemed to consider what Oray said. Then as Oray and the others noticed this and turned their attention to him, he spoke in a quiet and thoughtful voice.

"He'll be responsible for seven deaths soon."

The others watched Layton with sadness and compassion. Then Rizette moved over to his wheelchair and put her hand on his shoulder. Vance also moved over to his other shoulder and squeezed it in a gesture of support.

Hugh now spoke.

"Commissioner Redstone crossed the line of criminal activity years ago. The problem for the security system has been the absence of a living diver. Without a living diver in the creed, the security system could only gather evidence against the commissioner and put forth an effort to locate a qualified diver to enlist.

"Carl was one of the divers. Layton and Vance were also potential divers for the creed. Unfortunately, Commissioner Redstone, at this point, had wormed into the system far enough to know something was happening beyond the scope of his control. He was also able to make a loose connection with the divers that reached the level of 'A classification.' So, he tried to recruit divers who were coming into a class A position. These were, of course, also candidates to be recruited by the creed, though he had little real information about what the creed was. When he saw no success with these divers, he would get concerned about them gaining power through the creed entity and exposing his crimes. So, his solution was to throw them into a drift status and release notifications that these divers had been transferred to a top-secret and classified position."

Vance now added some insight. "That explains a lot. He wanted Carl, Layton, and I to help him track down a mysterious 'hostile faction.' But what he actually wanted all along was more information on the creed."

Jackson nodded and replied.

"Right. He only had fragments of information on the matter. As each of you came into a position to be recruited by the creed security system, he tried to get to you first. Of course, none of you except Oray made it through the process of the creed oath. So, when no information came to him, he simply made you disappear into the military training sequence. This was a sequence that only he held control over, so he believed it would eliminate you forever. But now, his crimes will be brought against him. With Oray in a position to trigger the final action, all of his illegal activities will come to light."

208

Layton now asked, "So why didn't you get with Oray before he became a drifter?"

Jackson appeared a little embarrassed but then replied. "It was one thing we didn't prepare for. It was assumed that once a diver took the oath and became a member of the creed, they would ask their assistant for information and access to the creed facilities. The foresight of a situation such as Oray found himself in was never considered. And diver assistants were only instructed to relay information as it was requested by the diver. It's unfortunate what the four of you have had to endure. The fact that you successfully made it here is itself a testament to your resilience and courage. This will be beneficial for the future of this facility."

Vance seemed concerned now.

"Yes, but we've been in the virtual zone far too long. We'll need physical therapy and time to recover. How can we take on Redstone in the condition we'll be in?"

Oray now replied. "We plan to do everything from the virtual zone."

Jackson stepped forward and continued from where Oray left off.

"Everything can be done from the station. We know when the commissioner enters the virtual zone as well as the council members. We want to initiate this as if the commissioner accidentally triggered a hidden security program leftover from the old-world, as you now call it. This is, in a sense, what he did.

"Everything will unfold to the council members in a way that reveals the commissioner went too far without the proper authority. This causes an information dump into the council members' data file. They will receive this information while in the virtual zone. They will also become notified of all the pod locations the commissioner has hidden. The system will automatically lock the commissioner's pod until the council members make their judgment."

Vance thought of this for a few seconds and then said. "So, none of the council members will know about the creed's existence?"

Oray replied.

"Vance, you were selected as a potential creed member long before me. After all of this settles down and we've fully recovered physically, Jackson and Hugh want you to join the creed."

Hugh stepped a little closer to Vance now.

"Vance, Jackson, and I would like for you and Oray to continue the work of the creed. We'll be here to help you both. But the system requirements demand actual living creed members to be in control. This is a good rule, and the creed should never be the tool of any criminal faction, be it living or virtual. With you and Oray as the new senior officers, the creed can again serve the purpose of protecting both divers and those who use the facilities, as it originally did long ago."

Vance gazed out into the now white room as he thought about this. Then he turned to Oray, Hugh, and Jackson.

"The creed saved us, even though we didn't know anything about it. I want the creed to continue. I'm in."

Everyone smiled and began to pat Vance and Oray on their shoulders as they all realized this to be the dawn of a new diver creed organization. Rizette hugged Oray, and they all moved back into the station together.

Now, time slowed down as the four awaited all the pieces to come into place. Hugh and Jackson would update them about the progress.

Commission Redstone entered the virtual zone at regular times. The situation needed for proper judicial proceedings would be a majority as well a one senior council member being in the virtual zone at the same time as the commissioner. Since the commissioner had put Councilwoman Leea and Councilman Henriys into a drift pattern, this brought the number down to four needed for judgment proceedings to take place.

They waited patiently as the proper pieces of the case came together.

After a week of lingering around the station, Jackson came to the Greek eating facility where Oray, Rizette, Vance, and Layton were enjoying a meal. They all turned to him as he approached.

"It's time," Jackson said without emotion.

The three stood up a little nervously. Vance got behind Layton's wheelchair, and they began to follow Jackson.

"You're sure he won't see us?" Layton asked.

"Neither Commissioner Redstone nor the council members will have any knowledge of our presence. They only received the information that the commissioner cast you into a drifting state along with the evidence of his other crimes. They've been given access retrieval codes to initiate your exits from the virtual zone.

"The drift locations of Rizette's Aunt Leea, as well as Councilman Henriys and his family have been located. These two and four other council members were brought together in the virtual zone and presented the evidence against the commissioner. They've discussed everything and decided on a verdict. What we'll witness is their meeting with the commissioner. At this point, he has no knowledge of his crimes having been brought to the council member's attention."

The six of them moved into the large, darkened doorway. As they walked forward, the scenery around them shifted, and they came into a large, luxurious room. Inside this room were an elaborate Jacuzzi and various other fine furnishings. Inside the Jacuzzi were Commissioner Redstone and four young women. They were all pretty, and some held drinks and laughed as the commissioner appeared to be playing and teasing them. He would kiss one on the neck and then move over to another one. Soft music played in the background.

The six visitors remained in a darkened corner of the room unseen. As this played out, several council members began to arrive; seeming to walk through the walls. As the seconds went by, more appeared, and soon, there were six council members quietly standing around the Jacuzzi.

One of the young women suddenly noticed the council members. She stopped laughing and moved away from the commissioner's grasp. This caused the other women to look and become shocked by the sudden appearance of the strangers. Then the commissioner turned and noticed the council members.

"What are you doing here? Get out, all of you. I'll have you all arrested," he said very aggressively.

Rizette's Aunt Leea then stepped from a darkened area. When the commissioner saw her, he became obviously unsettled. Then, Councilman Henriys also stepped from the darkness.

"Wha, what is this about? Why are you here?" His voice now had a nervous tone.

"We're here to arrest you, commissioner," Leea said.

"What are you talking about? What charges are you basing this on?"

"The charges are murder, kidnapping, extortion, and a host of other lesser charges."

When Councilwoman Leea said this, the young women began to get out of the Jacuzzi, grabbing towels to cover their naked bodies. They all left the room one by one until only the commissioner was alone in the Jacuzzi.

"You, you have no proof of this." The commissioner now became obviously unsettled.

"Control," Rizette's Aunt Leea called out.

"Yes, Councilwoman Leea 514."

"Present the evidence of crimes to the commissioner."

After Councilwoman Leea said this, an apparent flash of information passed into the commissioner's mind. He immediately appeared to be in pain due to the revelation. He put his hand to his head and strained at the obvious evidence available to the council members. He looked up at them and, in a stressed tone, asked.

"Where did you get this information? How did you get this information? Tell me!"

A male council member now answered him.

"You triggered a security system program leftover from the old-world controllers. This system was put into place to police criminal actions such as the ones you've committed. The only reason you've gotten away with it for so long is the access codes you used to restart the system were not of a high level. The security system was geared to monitor high-level officials. But your crimes have been so massive that the security system finally dumped the information to clean its data banks. Through this information dump, we not only have all the evidence of the crimes you've committed but also the location of the pods of those you've sent into drift mode. A retrieval code has also been connected to these drifters, and the survivors will be moved towards an available exit to disembark the virtual zone."

He paused briefly and then continued.

"From this information dump that you triggered, we've also discovered that punishment for crimes such as yours can be administered here in the virtual zone if a board of council members agrees upon the evidence of guilt. It's an old-world military punishment authorization and has the power to administer actual life sentences. After considering the matter, we've decided to deal with this situation here and now, commissioner. You're much too dangerous on the outside."

The commissioner now moved backward into the Jacuzzi. His face appeared pale and frightened.

"You can't do this. The virtual facility is mine. I'm the one with the access codes. I'm the one who reactivated the system. You can't do this. It's mine."

No one said anything for a few seconds. Then Councilwoman Leea answered the commissioner.

"Even if the facility were yours, commissioner, by using it to kill, you've still committed murder."

The council members now waited silently as if giving the commissioner one last chance to speak on his own behalf. He seemed dazed now, and though he acted as if he wanted to say something, he couldn't find any words of defense.

Layton and the others watched this play out from their unseen location. Rizette glanced down at Layton to see he appeared stern and focused on this judgment against the commissioner.

After a moment of quiet tension, the senior council member spoke, "Control."

"Yes, Councilman Josel 359."

"The board of council has viewed the evidence against Commissioner Redstone. We find him guilty of all crimes presented."

"What punishment has the board agreed upon?" the voice asked.

"Random punishment sequence for first-degree murder."

"Are all the board members in agreement with this?"

When the Control voice asked this, every council member stated their agreement. Commissioner Redstone now became very agitated and seemed to be searching for some way out as he moved around in the Jacuzzi, mumbling to himself.

"Punishment is authorized. Commissioner Redstone, you have been found guilty of first-degree murder by an authorized board of council members. You will receive a life sentence in a randomly selected sequence applicable to your crimes."

Now Commissioner Redstone reacted in panic.

"No, wait! You can't do this to me. Wait! We can sort this out...on the outside. You've got to give me more time!" As he said this, he moved about the Jacuzzi as a trapped animal might search in vain for an escape route.

"Goodbye, commissioner," Councilwoman Leea said. Then the council members turned to leave as the scene began to shift around the commissioner.

The Jacuzzi melted away and sounds of war began to blend into the changing environment. An army uniform and helmet materialized on the commissioner and around him developed a muddy trench. The sky became gray, and the smell of death and gunpowder filled the heavy air. A man who appeared to be the officer in charge walked up to the commissioner, who now sat huddled on a small wooden bench with a rifle between his legs. He appeared to be in shock as the officer moved past him, yelling out orders.

"We'll be going over the top in thirty seconds, everyone up and ready!" As the officer said this, the sound of a rapid-firing machine gun began to chatter violently close by. Then, several artillery shells landed very near, causing debris to land on top of Commissioner Redstone.

"Get up, soldier!" the officer yelled at the commissioner.

He looked up at the officer with a dazed and shocked expression.

"I said get up now, or I'll shoot you on the spot!" The officer then pulled a pistol from his holster.

Commissioner Redstone stood up weakly. Then a whistle blew somewhere along the line. Hundreds of soldiers began to crawl from the trench. The officer stood with pistol in hand until Commissioner Redstone slowly crawled out to the top of the trench. Machine gunfire erupted. Artillery shells landed all around. Then the scene faded from view.

"I've seen enough," Layton said.

From their darkened observation area on the battlefield, the group turned and began walking away. Then they moved into the large white room again and from there into the station.

Vance wheeled Layton to a rest area. Oray now turned to Hugh and Jackson.

"How much time do we have before the council retrieves us from our pods?"

"As much time as you want. The council members will input a search code that accompanies the info dump. The system will simply indicate it's searching the virtual zone for you until you decide to exit. A retrieval search of this sort could technically take two hours, two days, or even two weeks," Hugh replied.

"That's good. We would like to get Layton situated before exiting the virtual zone." When Oray said this, Rizette lowered her head a little. Then she moved closer to Oray and put her arm around his waist.

"Yes, that's understandable. As a member of the diver creed, you have complete access to the massive virtual zone sequence database. Take as much time as you need and do whatever you can to make him comfortable."

Oray and Rizette smiled and nodded when Hugh said this. Then they walked towards the rest area together, arm in arm.

After some rest, the four went to dinner. They ate and spoke of their experience with tears and laughter. For several hours, they relived the horrors and the triumph of their ordeal together. Then, as the conversation seemed to lose course, Oray turned and spoke to Layton.

"There's a sequence that Rizette and I are familiar with, Layton. It's beautiful and peaceful. We would like to show it to you."

Layton stared at his glass on the table. He then took it in his hand and raised it to take a drink. After sitting it back on the table, he rubbed his thumb up and down along the side of it as if in thought. Finally, he replied.

"Yes, I would like that. I'm glad you three will make it out. I never really had much of a family on the outside. Although the circumstances weren't great, I think the three of you have been the closest thing to a real family."

When Layton said this, Rizette began to cry. She turned her head away to hide her tears. Regardless, she couldn't keep from breaking down, and the others knew she wept.

Vance leaned over and put his hand on Layton's arm.

"You've been a great help in us reaching the station. Who knows how many people Redstone had wasting away in hidden pods? Not only will we survive, but many others will because of you, Layton."

Layton tried to smile. He nodded to Vance. Oray then put his hand on Layton's shoulder. Rizette wiped her tears away. She moved to the other side of Layton and put her arm around his shoulders, giving him a hug. They all sat in this way for a few minutes. The reality of their challenges in the virtual zone now fused into an unbreakable bond.

The following morning, Vance pushed Layton's wheelchair as they followed Oray into the large, darkened doorway. Once inside, the area lit up as before. Then the scene around them shifted into the beach Oray and Rizette had become fond of in their time off.

"So, what do you think?" Rizette knelt beside Layton as she asked him this.

"It's beautiful. I think I could get used to this."

They moved up to some beach chairs, and Vance helped Layton into one. Then, Oray pointed his finger down to a table beside Layton. A pair of sunglasses materialized where he pointed. Rizette was the only one who saw this, and she looked at Oray with obvious amazement. He smiled slyly and winked at her. Oray then picked up the glasses and handed them to Layton, who put them on as he leaned back into the beach chair.

Rizette squatted down beside him and put her arm on his shoulder.

"We'll come and visit you often."

He turned to her and smiled when she said this. Then put his hand on top of hers, and patting it, he said, "I would like that very much."

A waiter approached the group, and Oray walked a few steps to meet him before reaching the group.

"Bring him anything he wants. Check on him often. I want him to have the finest room in the hotel and the best of everything. Do you understand?"

The waiter looked at Oray and nodded. "Yes, sir, I understand." He then walked up to the others and bent down to Layton.

"May I interest you in a drink, sir, or maybe something to eat?"

Layton chuckled about this. "Now, this is what I call service." The others laughed as well.

After saying their goodbyes Oray, Rizette, and Vance began to leave. As they moved a few yards from where Layton sat, a beautiful blonde woman in a rather small bikini walked from the beach straight up to Oray. Rizette initially glanced over to her husband with a bit of suspicion in her eyes. But then she looked closer at the blonde woman and realized this was the same woman that Serri had hit, causing her to fall into the swimming pool and drown. When the woman stood directly in front of Oray he spoke to her as if expecting her to approach.

"Keep him company. Stay with him as long as he wants and stay close for when he wants company. Do you understand?"

"Yes, sir," the blonde woman said.

She then walked straight over to Layton and sat down in a chair beside him. She began to talk with him, and soon both were talking and laughing.

Rizette turned to Oray after they'd observed this for a few seconds.

"Isn't that?" She pointed to the blonde woman with Layton.

He smiled a little and nodded.

"She's the class B companion NLP from the rock star sequence. I remembered you telling me about her and thought Layton might appreciate her more than Serri did."

After watching the two for a few moments, they turned and left.

When they returned to the station, Hugh and Jackson met them in front of the large doorway.

They stood for a moment without saying anything. Then Vance spoke.

"Well, it'll be a while before we can come back. There's going to be some recovery time needed after this much time in the virtual zone." The others nodded in agreement. Vance continued.

"So, are we ready then?"

After a few seconds of thought, Oray said.

"There's one more thing I need to do before we exit."

Rizette looked at Oray curiously. Then seeming to understand him, she squeezed his arm and rubbed it slightly. Oray turned and walked back into the darkened doorway alone.

As he walked, everything around him shifted to a white room with lighting like the turnstile. Riley came into view, and Oray stopped before Riley noticed him.

He sat alone in the white room; his hands clasped over his legs. Oray wondered what his assistant was thinking of as he sat there staring at the floor in front of him.

Oray winced a little, and his gaze dropped to the floor as he painfully recalled the suspicions he had about his friend. Then he raised his head again and walked slowly towards Riley.

When Riley noticed Oray walking towards him in the gray suit of the diver creed, he immediately stood up and smiled.

"Sir, you're back! I'm so glad to see you!"

Oray smiled, and Riley immediately put his hand out for Oray to shake.

"You look, great sir. It seems certain you found the station. I'm so glad. I was very concerned."

After shaking Riley's hand, Oray spoke in a humbled tone.

"Yes, I found the station, thanks to you, Riley."

"Oh, no matter, sir. I've really missed working with you, sir. Will you be returning to work then?"

"Yes, I'll be returning to work as soon as my body recovers. I've been in the virtual zone a bit longer than I should have."

Riley laughed a little about this, and Oray did as well. Then Oray became serious. He looked down briefly and then back up and into Riley's eyes.

"Riley, I want to thank you for being so persistent about the creed. And I want to thank you for insisting on giving me the oath in a C6 junction point." Oray then paused and took hold of Riley's arm with his right hand and continued.

"But most of all, Riley, I want you to know how grateful I am to have you as a friend."

His assistant appeared to be at a loss for words when Oray said this. He seemed to be almost ready to cry, and Oray knew he'd done the right thing to come here and tell him this.

This realization caused Oray to smile. He gave Riley a quick hug. Riley finally regained his composure and spoke with much emotion in his voice.

"Well, I ...ah, you're, quite welcome, sir... and, I'm very grateful to have you as my friend as well."

The End

Thank you for reading Diver Creed Station. We hope you enjoyed it. For your convenience we've listed other books by Oliver Phipps that you may enjoy. Please check out all of Oliver Phipps' books online.

SPYDER BONES

We've heard the tales. The eternal struggle between good and evil. Many religions are based on the concepts. God, Satan, angels and demons; ideals interwoven into our very existence.

Most all have chosen a side, whether they admit it to themselves or not. Many have at least a basic understanding of what is happening. Some have even discovered secrets beyond the veil of what we see. However, there are a few, who not only understand the war, but are in the very thick of it.

This is the story of Spyder Bones, a mystic warrior.

It's the summer of 1969 and Aaron Prescott is a seasoned soldier. After serving one tour of duty in Vietnam as a cavalryman, Aaron returns for a second tour as a combat medic.

Aaron's life revolves around the love of his Vietnamese girlfriend, the danger of combat and his passion for music. It's not an overly complicated existence. But that's about to change.

Aaron, or Spyder as he is known to his friends, suffers a near death experience during combat. He is subsequently trapped in a comatose state for months. During this time, he is exposed to an unseen war. A spiritual struggle that most only have a vague awareness of.

Aaron must make some difficult decisions. But, regardless of anything else, he knows his life will never be the same.

WHERE THE STRANGERS LIVE

When a passenger plane disappears over the Indian Ocean in autumn 2013, a massive search gets underway.

A deep-trolling, unmanned pod picks up faint readings and soon the deep-sea submersible Oceana and her three crew members are four miles below the ocean surface in search of the black box from flight N340.

Nothing could have prepared the submersible crew for what they discover and what happens afterwards. Ancient evils and other world creatures challenge the survival of the Oceana's crew. Mysteries of the past are revealed, but death hangs in the balance for Sophie, Troy and Eliot in this deep-sea Science Fiction thriller.

TEARS OF ABANDON

Several college friends start planning a two week kayak trip down an Alaskan river in late summer of 1992. Soon there are five young people headed to Alaska for a river expedition.

As the trip unfolds and the group gets farther into the wilderness a strange whispering sound attracts their attention. The wonderful vacation begins to take a turn for the worse when they follow the sounds and find something long lost and quite unexpected.

This thrilling story from the author of The House on Cooper Lane and A Tempest Soul has it all, Alaska, ghosts and gold.

BANE OF THE INNOCENT

"There's no reason for them to shoot us; we ain't anyone" - Sammy, Bane of the Innocent.

Two young boys become unlikely companions during the fall of Atlanta. Sammy and Ben somehow find themselves, and each other, in the rapidly changing and chaotic environment of the war-torn Georgia City.

As the siege ends and the fall begins in late August and early September of 1864 the Confederate troops begin to move out and Union forces cautiously move into the city. Ben and Sammy simply struggle to survive, but in the process, they develop a friendship that will prove more important than either one could imagine.

TWELVE MINUTES TILL MIDNIGHT

A man catches a ride on a dusty Louisiana road only to find out he's traveling with notorious outlaws Bonnie and Clyde.

The suspense is nonstop as confrontation settles in between a man determined to stand on truth and an outlaw determined to dislocate him from it.

If your life is subject to living a lie rather than holding to the truth, which would you do?

"Twelve Minutes till Midnight will take you on an unforgettable ride."

GHOSTS OF COMPANY K

Tag along with young Bud Fisher during his daily adventures in this ghostly tale based on actual events. It's 1971 and Bud and his family move into an old house in Northern Arkansas. Bud soon discovers they live not far from a very interesting cave as well as a historic Civil War battle site. As odd things start to happen, Bud tries to solve the mysteries. But soon the entire family experiences a haunting situation.

If you enjoy ghost tales based on true events, then you'll enjoy Ghosts of Company K. This heartwarming story brings the reader into the life and experiences of a young boy growing up in the early 1970s. Seen through innocent and unsuspecting eyes, Ghosts of Company K reveals a haunting tale from the often-unseen perspective of a young boy.

THE HOUSE ON COOPER LANE

It's 1984 and all Bud Fisher wants to do is find a place to live in Madison Louisiana. With his dog Badger, they come across a beautiful old mansion that was converted into apartments.

Something should have felt odd when he found out nobody lived in any of the apartments. To make matters worse, the owner is reluctant to let him rent one. Eventually he negotiates an apartment in the historic old house, but soon finds out that he's not quite as alone as he thought. What ghostly secret has the owner failed to share?

It's up to Bud to unravel the mysteries of the upstairs apartments, but is he really ready to find out the truth?

A TEMPEST SOUL

Seventeen-year-old Gina Falcone has been alone for much of her young life. Her father passed away while she was young. Her unaffectionate mother eventually leaves her to care for herself when she is only thirteen.

Though her epic journey begins in 1920 by an almost deadly mistake, Gina will find many of her heart's desires in the most unlikely of places. The loss of everything is the catalyst that brings her to an unimagined level of accomplishment in her life.

Yet Gina soon realizes it is the same events that brought her success that may also bring everything crashing down around her. The new life she has built soon beckons for something she left behind. Now the new woman must find a way to dance through a life she could have never dreamed of.

A LIFE NAIVE

Life for twenty-seven-year-old Hershel Lawson has been relatively uneventful and that's the way he likes it. When his grandmother passes away, leaving him her car and a last wish of him taking her ashes to L.A., his life takes a turn and it will never be the same again.

With his new task and grandmother's ashes, Hershel sets out from St. Louis Missouri in the spring of 1962. He travels unimpeded along scenic Route 66 for two days but is suddenly and unexpectedly relieved of two important things, his car and wallet.

Sally is a sassy and street-smart young woman on her way to Hollywood. She's determined to prove everyone wrong in the "one horse town" she left and make it as an actress in California. Through mishaps of her own, Sally comes across Hershel. Though neither one realizes it, the real journey is about to begin.

Take a seat and journey with Hershel and Sally along historic Route 66 during its heyday. Laugh and maybe shed a tear or two as they struggle against the odds, and often each other, to make it a few more miles down the highway.

THE BITTER HARVEST

The year is 1825, and a small Native American village has lost many of its people and bravest warriors to a pack of Lofa; huge beasts' humanoid in shape but covered with coarse hair. The creatures are taller than any normal man, and fiercer than even the wildest animal.

Rather than leave the land of their ancestors, the tribe chooses to stay and fight the beasts. But they're losing the war, and perhaps more critically, they're almost without hope.

The small community grasps for anything to help them survive. There is a warrior on the frontier known as Orenda. He's already legendary across the west for his bravery and honor.

Onsi, a young villager, sets out on a journey to find the warrior.

Orenda will be forced to choose between almost certain death, not just for himself, but also his warrior wife Nazshoni and her brother Kanuna, or a dishonorable refusal that would mean annihilation for the entire village.

The crucial decision is only the beginning, and Orenda will soon face the greatest test of his life; the challenge that could turn out to be too much even for a warrior of legend.